TOM SAWYER

Globe Book Company, Inc.

Englewood Cliffs, New Jersey

MARK TWAIN

TOM SAWYER

Adapted by
Erwin H. Schubert

Edited by
Delpha Hurlburt

Reading Consultant
M. Jerry Weiss

An
Adapted
Classic

Erwin H. Schubert

formerly Head of the English Department
West Milwaukee High School
Milwaukee, Wisconsin

Delpha Hurlburt

formerly Director of the Educational Clinic
Pacific University
Forest Grove, Oregon

M. Jerry Weiss

Distinguished Service Professor of Communication
Jersey City State College
Jersey City, New Jersey

Illustrations: Ted Burwell
Cover Design: Art Ritter
Cover Illustration: Ted Burwell

Third Edition 1987

ISBN: 0-87065-009-2

Printed in the United States of America 11 12 13 14 15 16

Globe Book Company
A Division of Simon & Schuster
Englewood Cliffs, New Jersey

ABOUT THE AUTHOR

Mark Twain, or Samuel Langhorne Clemens, was born in Florida, Missouri, in 1835. He took his writing name "Mark Twain" from the call of the sounders on the front of the big Mississippi and Missouri River steamboats. The sounders were men who tested the depth of the water so that the big flat-bottomed boats wouldn't run aground on the sand bars. "Mark Twain" was the call for two fathoms, or twelve feet. This was the depth the boats needed to stay afloat. Clemens first used the name in 1862 while working for a newspaper.

Mark Twain was not even three years old when his family moved to Hannibal, Missouri, on the Mississippi River. He held jobs as a printer, steamboat pilot, prospector, adventurer, reporter, writer, lecturer, editor, humorist, traveler, and critic. Many of the scenes, events, and people in *The Adventures of Tom Sawyer* were based on Twain's own experiences as a steamboat pilot and resident of Hannibal.

Some of Mark Twain's other books are: *The Adventures of Huckleberry Finn, The Prince and the Pauper, A Connecticut Yankee at King Arthur's Court, Life on the Mississippi, Innocents Abroad, Pudd'n'head Wilson,* and the *Autobiography of Mark Twain.*

Mark Twain died in Redding, Connecticut, in 1910. He is often called the greatest American humorist.

PREFACE

This is the story of a boy who lived in a small town on the Mississippi River over 100 years ago. Can you imagine what life was like then? There were no movies, TVs, or stereos. There were no cars, motorcycles, or planes. There were no air conditioners, electric lights, or refrigerators. But there was adventure.

In the following pages you will meet the people who lived in this small town. Some of these people will make you think of people you really know. Their lives may be different from yours, but many of their problems are the same. They may speak differently, but they have many of the same thoughts as you do. And many of the things that made people laugh 100 years ago will make you laugh today.

ADAPTER'S NOTE

In preparing this edition of *The Adventures of Tom Sawyer,* we have tried to keep Mark Twain's main purpose in mind. Since Tom Sawyer was published in 1876, however, language has changed. We have modified or omitted some passages and some vocabulary. We have, however, kept as much of the original as possible.

CONTENTS

TOM SAWYER

1 Tom Skips Out
—And In

"Tom!"

No answer.

"TOM!"

No answer.

"Where *is* that boy, I wonder? YOU, TOM!"

The old lady pulled her eyeglasses down and looked over them around the room. Then she put them up and looked out under them. She seldom or never looked *through* them for so small a thing as a boy. She looked puzzled for a moment, and then said:

"Well, if I get hold of you I'll—!"

She did not finish, for by this time she was bending down and punching under the bed with the broom. She stirred up nothing but the cat.

"I never did see the like of that boy!"

She went to look out the doorway. No Tom. So she lifted up her voice to aim for distance and shouted:

"YOU-U-U, TOM!"

There was a slight noise behind her. She turned just in time to seize a small boy by the loose end of his jacket and stop his flight.

"There! I might have thought of that closet. What have you been doing in there?"

"Nothing."

"Nothing! Look at your hands—and look at your mouth! What *is* that stuff?"

"I don't know, aunt."

"Well, *I* know. It's jam—that's what it is! Forty times

1

I've told you, if you didn't let that jam alone, I'd skin you. Hand me that stick!"

"My! Look behind you, auntie!"

The old lady whirled around. The lad fled, on the instant, climbed up the high board fence of the back yard, and disappeared over it.

Tom's Aunt Polly stood surprised a moment, and then broke into a gentle laugh.

"That boy! Can't I ever learn anything? He's played enough tricks on me like that for me to be looking out for him by this time! But my goodness, he never plays two alike, and how is a body to know what's coming? But he's my own dead sister's boy, and I haven't the heart to whip him. He'll stay out, now, a long time, and I'll be obliged to make him work, tomorrow, to punish him. It's mighty hard to make him work Saturdays, when all the boys are out playing, but he hates work more than he hates anything else, and I've *got* to do my duty or I'll spoil him."

Tom did stay out, and he had a very good time. He got back home just in time to help Jim, the young black handyman, saw the wood for the next day. At least, Tom was there in time to tell his adventures to Jim while Jim did three-fourths of the work. Tom's younger brother (or rather, half brother), Sid, was already finished with his work of picking up the chips, for Sid was a quiet boy, and had no daring ways.

While Tom was eating his supper, and stealing extra sugar whenever he could, Aunt Polly asked him questions to find out if he had been in school all day. Said she:

"Tom, it was warm in school, wasn't it?"

"Yes'm."

"Very warm, wasn't it?"

"Yes'm."

"Didn't you want to go swimming, Tom?"

A bit of fear shot through Tom. Did she know? He searched Aunt Polly's face, but it told him nothing. So he said:

"No'm. Well, not very much."

The old lady reached out her hand and felt Tom's shirt, and said:

"But you aren't too warm now, though!"

"Some of us pumped water on our heads. Mine is damp yet, see?"

"Tom, you didn't have to open your shirt collar where I sewed it, to pump water on your head, did you? Open your jacket!"

Tom opened his jacket. His shirt collar was still sewed.

"Well, all right! I thought surely you hadn't been in school all day, but had been swimming. But, I forgive you, Tom, *this* time."

But Sidney said:

"Well, now, I thought you sewed his collar with white thread—but, it's black!"

"Why, I did sew it with white! Tom!"

But Tom did not wait—he went out the door. As he left he said:

"Siddy, I'll beat you for that!"

In a safe place Tom examined the thread. It was black. He said to himself:

"She would never have noticed it if it hadn't been for Sid! Sometimes she sews it with white, and sometimes she sews it with black. I wish she would stick to one or the other! *I* can't keep track of 'em. But I'll get Sid for that!"

Within two minutes, or even less, Tom had forgotten all his troubles. He was interested in a new way of whistling that sounded like a bird. After a little practice, he learned it, and went whistling down the street with his mouth full of music.

The evening was early. It was not dark, yet. Presently Tom checked his whistle. A stranger was before him. It was a boy, a little larger than himself, who had just moved into the village.

Tom looked him over. The boy was well dressed. He wore a cap and a new blue jacket. He had shoes on— and it was only Friday. He even wore a necktie. He looked like a city boy.

Neither boy spoke. If one moved, the other moved —but only sideways, in a circle. They kept face to face and eye to eye all the time. Finally Tom said:

"I can lick you!"

"I'd like to see you try it!"

"Well, I can do it."

"No you can't."

"Yes I can."

"You can't."

"I can."

"Can't."

There was a pause. Then Tom said:

"What's your name?"

"It's none of your business."

"Well, I'll *make* it my business!"

"Well, why don't you?"

"If you say much, I will!"

"Much—much—*much*! There, now!"

"Oh, you think you're mighty smart, *don't* you? I could lick you with one hand tied behind me, if I wanted to!"

"Well, why don't you *do* it? You *say* you can do it."

"Well, I *will*, if you fool with me."

"Well, why don't you *do* it then? What do you keep *saying* you will for? Why don't you *do* it. It's because you're afraid!"

"I'm not afraid."

"You are!"

"I'm not."

"You are!"

There was another pause, and more moving

around. Presently they were shoulder to shoulder. Tom said:

"Get away from here!"

"Get away yourself!"

"I won't."

"*I* won't either!"

Tom drew a line in the dust and said:

"I dare you to step over that, and I'll lick you till you can't stand up!"

The new boy stepped over the line at once, and said:

"Let's see you do it!"

"Don't you crowd me now. You better look out!"

"Well, you *said* you'd do it! Why don't you do it?"

"By jingo! For two cents I *will* do it!"

The new boy took two pennies out of his pocket and held them out. Tom struck them to the ground. In an instant both boys were rolling and fighting in the dirt. For a minute they tugged, tore, punched, and scratched at each other. Presently, from the mix-up, Tom appeared, seated on the new boy, and pounding him with his fists.

"Holler 'enough'!" said Tom.

The boy only struggled to free himself. He was crying—mainly from rage.

"Holler 'enough'!"

The pounding went on.

At last the stranger got out a weak "Enough!" and Tom let him up and said:

"Now, that'll teach you! Better look out who you're fooling with, next time!"

The new boy went off brushing the dust from his clothes and crying that he'd get even with Tom. Tom only made fun of him, and started for home. But, as soon as his back was turned, the new boy picked up a stone, threw it, and hit Tom between the shoulders. Then the new boy turned and ran like a deer.

Tom chased him home, and thus found out where the new boy lived. Tom waited at the gate for some time, daring the enemy to come outside, but the enemy only made faces at him through the window. At last the boy's mother appeared, called Tom a bad boy, and ordered him to go away. So he went away, but Tom said he'd "get" that new boy.

Tom got home pretty late, that night. As he tried to sneak in through a window, Aunt Polly caught him. When she saw his clothes from the fight, she made up her mind to put him to work all the next day, Saturday.

2 *Work Is Turned Into Play*

Saturday morning came, bright, summery, and with no school. There was a song in every heart.

Tom appeared on the sidewalk with a bucket of whitewash and a big brush. He looked at the fence, thirty yards of board nine feet high, and all gladness left him. Sighing, he wet his brush and painted the top board. He painted another—and then looked at the long way to go. He sat down, ready to give up.

Jim came out at the gate with a tin pail, and singing. He was on his way to the town pump to get water. Tom had always hated getting water, but he forgot his hate now. He remembered that there was company at the pump, and excitement. Tom said:

"Say, Jim, I'll go and get the water if you'll whitewash some."

Jim shook his head and said:

"Can't, Tom. Old Miss Polly told me to get the water and not fool around with anybody. She said she expected you to ask me to whitewash, and she told me to go along and attend to my own business. She said *she* would take care of the whitewashing."

"Oh, never mind what she said, Jim. That's the way she always talks. Give me the bucket—I won't be gone only a minute. *She* won't ever know."

"Oh, I don't dare, Tom. She'd take my head off, indeed she would!"

"*She!* She never licks anybody—hits 'em over the head with her thimble—and who cares for that, I'd like to know. She talks awful, but talk doesn't hurt. Jim, I'll give you a marble—a white alley!"

Jim became interested.

"A white alley, Jim! Besides, I'll show you my sore toe."

Jim was only human—this was too much for him. He put down his pail, took the marble, and bent over to look at the toe. In another moment he was flying down the street with his pail, Tom was working hard, and Aunt Polly was going back into the house with the slipper she had used!

But Tom's work did not last. He began to think of the fun he had planned for this day, and then of the work he had to do. He became sad. He knew that soon the boys would come along and make fun of him for having to work. He looked in his pockets to see what he had to trade to get someone to do his work. There wasn't enough. Then, at this dark moment, he got a bright idea!

He took up his brush and went back to work. Ben Rogers, the very boy who would make the most fun of him, came in sight, presently, with a hop, skip, and jump. Ben was eating an apple and making believe he was a steamboat, *and* the captain, *and* the engine, *and* the bells. But Tom went right on whitewashing—paid no attention to the steamboat. Ben stared a moment and then said:

"Hi-*yi*! *You're* up a stump, aren't you?!"

Tom didn't answer. He looked at his last touch with the eye of an artist. Then he gave another sweep of the brush and stopped to look at his stroke, as before. Ben moved up beside him. Tom's mouth watered for the apple, but he stuck to his work. Ben said:

"Hello, old chap. You've got to work, hey?"

Tom wheeled suddenly and said:

"Why, it's you, Ben! I didn't notice."

"Say—*I'm* going swimming, *I* am. Don't you wish you could? But of course *you'd* rather work—course you would!"

Tom looked at Ben a while, then said:

"I like it. Does a boy get a chance to whitewash a fence *every* day?"

That put the work in a new light. Ben stopped eating his apple. Tom swept the brush lightly back and forth—stepped back to look at the result—added a touch here and there. Ben watched every move, getting more and more interested. At last he said:

"Say, Tom, let *me* whitewash a little."

Tom considered, was about to consent, but changed his mind.

"No—no, I can't let you, Ben. You see, Aunt Polly is awful particular about *this* fence. If it were the back fence it would be all right. But, this front one has got to be done very carefully. I guess there isn't one boy in a thousand, maybe two thousand, that can do it the way it's got to be done!"

"No—is that so? Oh, come, now—let me just try —just a little. I'd let *you*, if you were me, Tom."

"Ben, I'd like to, honest Injun. But, Aunt Polly— well, Jim wanted to do it, but she wouldn't let him. Sid wanted to do it, and she wouldn't let Sid. Now don't you see how I'm fixed? If anything should happen to this fence—"

"Oh, shucks, I'll be careful. Now, let me try. Say— I'll give you the core of my apple."

"Well—no, Ben. I'm afraid—"

"I'll give you *all* of it!"

Tom gave up the brush as if he didn't want to, but

with cheer and consent in his heart. And while Ben worked and burned in the sun, Tom sat on a barrel in the shade eating Ben's apple—and planning new traps.

There was no lack of material, for boys came along every little while. They came to poke fun—but stayed to whitewash. When Ben was tired out, Tom traded the next chance to Billy Fisher for a kite. When *he* played out, Johnny Miller bought in for a dead rat—and so on, hour after hour.

The middle of the afternoon came. Tom was rolling in wealth. He had twelve marbles, a piece of blue glass to look through, a wooden gun, a key that wouldn't unlock anything, a mouth organ, a piece of chalk, a glass bottle closer, a tin soldier, two little frogs, six firecrackers, a kitten with only one eye, a brass doorknob, a dog collar, the handle of a knife, four orange peelings, and a ruined old window sash. And the fence had three coats of whitewash on it!

Tom said to himself that it was not such a bad world, after all. He had found a great law of human action. In order to make a man or boy want a thing, it is only necessary to make it hard to get.

The boy thought over, for a while, the big change which had taken place, and then went into the house to report.

3 Tom Falls in Love —Again

Tom presented himself before Aunt Polly, who was sitting by an open window, nearly asleep, over her knitting. She thought, of course, that Tom had deserted long ago, and was surprised to see him. He said:

"May I go and play now, aunt?"

"What! Already? How much have you done?"

"It's all done, aunt."

"Tom, don't lie to me—I can't bear it."

"I'm not, aunt. It *is* all done!"

Aunt Polly had to make sure—she went out to see for herself. When she found the entire fence whitewashed, and not only coated but painted several times, she could hardly say:

"Well, I never! There's no getting around it, Tom, you *can* work when you want to." Then she added, "But it's seldom you want to, I must say. Well, go along and play. But, mind you, get back some time in a week, or I'll tan you!"

She was so overcome by his splendid work that she gave him a choice apple. She delivered it to him with a talk on how good things could taste if they were earned. While she spoke, he "hooked" a doughnut.

Then he skipped out, and saw Sid outside. Pieces of clay were handy and the air was soon full of them directed at Sid. Before Aunt Polly could rescue Sid, six or seven pieces hit him, and Tom was over the fence and gone. There *was* a gate, but Tom never used it when he needed time. He was happy, now that he had settled with Sid for telling about the black thread.

Tom skirted the block to get safely beyond the reach of capture and punishment. Then he hastened toward the public square of the village. Here two armies of boys were met for battle according to an earlier plan. Tom was general of one of these armies. His good friend, Joe Harper, was general of the other. These two great officers were above fighting in person—that was left for the soldiers—they sat on a hill and gave the orders.

Tom's army won a great victory, after a long and hard battle. Then the dead were counted, prisoners exchanged, and the terms and the day for the next battle agreed upon. The armies then formed a line and marched away, and Tom turned homeward alone.

As he was passing Jeff Thatcher's house, he saw a new girl in the garden—a lovely little blue-eyed angel with golden hair. Tom fell in love with her at once, forgetting all about a certain Amy Lawrence, his old girl friend.

He worshiped this new angel with secret eye, till he saw that she had discovered him. Then he made believe he did not know she was present and began to show off. He turned cartwheels and was in the midst of standing on his head when he glanced aside and saw that she was going toward the house.

Tom came up to the fence and leaned on it. He was sad. He hoped she would stay longer. She stopped a moment on the steps and then moved toward the door. Tom sighed as she put her foot in the doorway, but his face lighted up as she turned and tossed a flower over the fence a moment before she disappeared.

Tom ran around the fence corner and stopped within a foot or two of the flower. Then he made believe he was interested in something going on down the street. Presently he picked up a straw and tried to balance it on his nose, moving nearer and nearer the flower. Finally his bare foot rested on it, his toes picked it up, and he hopped away around the corner with it. Within a minute he had buttoned the flower inside his jacket next his heart—or next his stomach—he didn't know.

He returned, now, and hung around the fence till dark, showing off, as before. But the girl never showed herself again. Tom felt sure, though, that she had been near some window and had seen him. Finally he floated home, with his poor head full of dreams.

All through supper his spirits were high. He didn't mind the good scolding he got for throwing at Sid. Aunt Polly wondered what had gotten into him, but when he tried to steal sugar from under her very nose, he got his knuckles rapped for it. Tom complained:

"Aunt, you don't hit Sid when he takes it!"

"Well, Sid doesn't tease the way you do. You'd always be in that sugar if I didn't watch you."

She stepped into the kitchen, and Sid, happy in his glory, reached for the sugar bowl. But Sid's fingers slipped and the bowl dropped and broke. Then Tom was happy. He said to himself he wouldn't speak a word until Aunt Polly asked who did it. Then he would tell and Sid would catch it.

He was full of joy and could hardly hold himself when the old lady came back, stood over the broken bowl, and glared angrily over her eyeglasses. Tom said to himself, "Now Sid's going to get it!" But, the next instant *he* was tossing on the floor!

Tom cried out:

"Hold on, now, what are you hitting *me* for? Sid broke it!"

Troubled, Aunt Polly paused. Tom looked for pity, but when she got her tongue again, she only said:

"Umpf! Well, you've been into some other mischief when I wasn't around, like enough!"

Then she felt bad and wanted to say something kind and loving, but she judged it best to keep silent. Tom sat in a corner and felt sorry for himself. He saw himself lying sick and dying and his aunt bending over him asking him to forgive her. But he would turn his face to the wall and die with that word unsaid. He imagined himself brought home from the river, dead—how sorry she would be, then. Even if she would promise never, never to treat him badly any more he would lie there cold and white and make no sign.

He so worked upon his feelings that the tears came and ran down and off the end of his nose. He wanted nothing but sorrow, and refused cheer. And so, presently, when his cousin, Mary, danced in happy to be home after a visit to the country, he got up and moved his sorrow out one door as she brought happiness in at the other.

He wandered from places boys usually were and sought to be alone with his feelings. A log raft in the river invited him, and he seated himself on its edge. He wished that he were drowned, without having to go through it, however.

Then he thought of his flower. He got it out, crushed and wilted. He wondered if *she* would pity him if *she* knew? Or would she turn coldly away? This idea brought him so much pleasant suffering that he thought it over and over again till he wore it out. At last he rose up sighing and departed in the darkness.

Later he came along the deserted street to where

the new girl lived. He paused. A light cast a dull glow upon the curtain of a second floor window. Was *she* there?

He climbed the fence, tiptoed under that window, and looked up at it a long time with much feeling. Then he lay on the ground on his back, his hands folded upon his breast and holding his poor dried flower. And thus he would die—out in the cold world. And thus *she* would see him when she looked out in the morning! Would she cry, or sigh?

The window went up. A maid's harsh voice broke the calm of the night—and a stream of water flooded over Tom!

The choking hero sprang up. There was a whiz as if something were being thrown through the air. A sound of breaking glass followed, and a small, dim form jumped over the fence and ran away in the dark.

Not long after, as Tom, all undressed for bed, was looking over his wet clothes in the room he shared with Sid, Sid woke up. If Sid had any dim idea of saying anything about appearances, he thought better of it and held his peace, for there was danger in Tom's eye.

Tom turned in without saying his prayers, and Sid made a note of the neglect.

4 Sunday School Comes —And Goes

It was Sunday. The sun rose upon a calm world and beamed down upon the peaceful village like a blessing. Breakfast over, Aunt Polly held family worship that she started with a long, solid prayer and topped with a grim sermon on one of the Ten Commandments from the Bible.

Then Tom "girded up his loins," as the Bible says, and went to work to get his lesson for Sunday School. Sid had learned his lesson days before. Tom chose a part of the Sermon on the Mount, the shortest verses he could find.

At the end of half an hour of study, Tom still didn't know the lesson because he had been thinking of other things. His cousin, Mary, took his book to hear him recite. He tried to find his way through the fog:

"Blessed are the—a—a—"

"Poor—"

"The poor—blessed are the poor—a—a—"

"In spirit—"

"In spirit—blessed are the poor in spirit, for they—a—they—"

"*Theirs*—"

"For *theirs*. Blessed are the poor in spirit, for *theirs* is the kingdom of heaven. Blessed are they that mourn, for they—a—they—"

"Sh—"

"For they—a—"

"S, H, A—"

"For they S, H—oh, I don't know what it is! Why don't you tell me, Mary? What do you want to be so mean for?!"

"Oh, Tom, I'm not teasing you. I wouldn't do that. You must go and learn it again—and if you do, I'll give you something nice. There, now, that's a good boy."

"All right! What is it, Mary? Tell me what it is."

"Never mind, Tom. You know if I say it's nice, it *is* nice."

"All right, Mary, I'll tackle it again."

And he did—under the double pressure of curiosity and future gain, he was a shining success. Mary gave him a brand-new single-bladed knife, the kind all the boys in town wanted. Tom was delighted. He began to carve on the cupboard with it, and was arranging to begin on the bureau when he was called to dress for Sunday School.

Mary gave him a basin of water and a piece of soap. He went outside on the porch, set the basin on a little bench there, and dipped the soap in the water. But he didn't wash with it. Instead, he laid the soap down, turned up his sleeves, and poured the water on the ground, gently.

Tom then entered the kitchen and began to wipe his face diligently on the towel behind the door. But Mary removed the towel and said:

"Now, aren't you ashamed, Tom! Water won't hurt you."

Tom was a bit disturbed. The basin was refilled. He stood over it awhile, gathering resolution, then took a big breath and began washing.

When he re-entered the kitchen with both eyes shut and groping for the towel with his hands, there was proof of suds and water dripping from his face. But when he emerged from the towel, he was not yet satisfactory, for the clean territory stopped at his chin. His ears and neck were still black.

Then Mary took him in hand. Soon his hair was neatly brushed and his short curls daintily waved. (But later Tom flattened the curls and plastered his hair close to his head because he thought his curls made him look like a girl.) Then Mary brought out his Sunday suit and after Tom had dressed himself she finished the job of turning his shirt collar over his coat, brushing him off, and putting on his head his speckled straw hat.

Tom now looked better, but felt miserable. He hoped that Mary would forget his stiff Sunday shoes, but she brought them out neatly polished. Tom lost his temper and said that he was always being made to do everything he didn't want to do. But Mary said:

"Please, Tom—be a good boy."

So he got into the shoes snarling. Mary was soon ready, and the three children set out for Sunday School —a place that Tom hated with his whole heart but Sid and Mary liked.

At the church door Tom dropped back to stop a friend and trade a piece of licorice, a fishhook, and a couple of white marbles for yellow, red, and blue tickets. He stopped other boys as they came for ten or fifteen minutes longer to buy more tickets. At last he entered the church.

In his seat, Tom started a quarrel with the first boy that came handy. When the man teacher stopped him, Tom waited until his back was turned, then pulled a boy's hair in the next row. When the boy turned around, Tom made believe he was reading his book. Then the same boy stuck a pin in another boy to hear him say

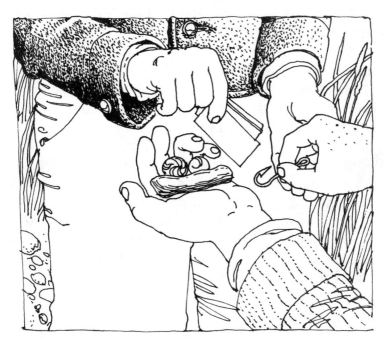

"Ouch!"—but when the teacher turned Tom was blamed.

As a reward for coming to Sunday School and reciting two verses, each child got a blue ticket. Ten blue tickets were worth a red one. Ten red tickets equaled a yellow one, and for ten yellow tickets a Bible was given. Mary had earned two Bibles. Tom had none, but he wanted the glory that came with it.

Soon the superintendent, Mr. Walters, began the Sunday School by saying:

"Now, children, I want you all to sit up straight and give me all your attention. There—that's it—that's the way good little boys and girls should do. But I see one little girl looking out of the window—I'm afraid she thinks I'm out there up in the trees making a speech to the little birds! I want to tell you how good it makes me feel to see so many bright, clean little faces here learning to do right and be good."

Mr. Walters didn't stop here, but kept on and on until everyone got tired listening to his speech, even Sid and Mary. At last the end of the speech came, at about the same time visitors entered, among them a gentleman, a lady, and a girl.

Tom saw that the girl was his angel of the garden, the new girl. The next moment he was "showing off" with all his might—he cuffed boys, pulled hair, made faces—he did everything to get the girl to notice him.

Mr. Walters introduced the visitors. The gentleman was Judge Thatcher, the lady was his wife, and the girl his daughter. With such an important person as a judge for a visitor, soon everyone was showing off— Mr. Walters, the teachers, the children—even the Judge himself, who was given a seat on the platform.

There was only one thing lacking to make Mr. Walters' happiness complete—a chance to give away a Bible and show off a smart child. But, he couldn't think of anyone who had enough tickets.

At this moment Tom Sawyer came forward with nine yellow tickets, nine red tickets, and ten blue ones, and demanded a Bible. Mr. Walters was thunderstruck —he had not expected Tom to get a Bible for the next ten years! But the tickets were there—and they were good.

Tom was placed next to the Judge and the great news was flashed to the Sunday School. Then everyone was surprised. But most of the boys knew that Tom had gotten the tickets by trading with them. They hated themselves for being tricked.

Mr. Walters gave Tom a Bible. The superintendent made a speech, but, he could not say very much. He was sure there was something wrong, for Tom would have had to learn two thousand verses. He felt sure that Tom would be strained by learning a dozen.

But Amy Lawrence was proud and glad. She tried to make Tom look so he could see it in her face. He wouldn't look. She wondered why—until she saw him looking at the new girl. Then Amy's heart broke. She was jealous, and angry. The tears came—she hated everybody, Tom most of all.

Tom was introduced to the Judge. The Judge put his hand on Tom's head and called him a fine little man, and asked him what his name was. Tom's tongue was tied, his breath would hardly come, his heart jumped—mainly because the Judge was *her* father. At last he got his name out:

"T-T-Tom!"

"Oh, no, not 'Tom'—it is—"

"Thomas."

"Ah, that's it. That's a good boy. Two thousand verses is a great many—and we are proud of little boys that learn. Now, won't you tell me and this lady some of the things you've learned? No doubt you know the names of all the twelve disciples. Won't you tell us the names of the first two that were called?"

Tom tugged at a buttonhole and looked sheepish. He blushed, now, and his eyes fell. Mr. Walters' heart sank within him, yet he spoke up and said:

"Answer the gentleman, Thomas—don't be afraid."

Tom still didn't answer.

"Now, I know you'll tell *me*," said the lady. "The names of the first two disciples were—"

"David and the Giant!"

Let us be kind—and draw the curtains over the rest of the scene!

5 Church Has Variety in It

Sunday School over, the bell of the small church was rung to call the people for the morning sermon. The children scattered themselves about the church to take seats with their parents. Aunt Polly came, and Tom, Sid, and Mary sat with her, but Tom was placed next to the aisle, away from the windows, so that he couldn't look out.

A crowd soon filled the church: the postmaster, the mayor and his wife, the justice of the peace, the rich widow Mrs. Douglas, the old soldier, Major Ward and Mrs. Ward, the lawyer, the belle of the village followed by many young fellows, and then the young clerks who admired the girls. Last of all came the model boy, Willie Mufferson, who was so good and polite that all the other boys didn't like him because he was held up as an example.

The church bell was rung once more, to warn the people, especially the late comers, that the services were about to begin. A solemn hush fell upon the church. The minister gave the number of the hymn and the song was sung. Then the reverend read the notices, or announcements.

And now the minister prayed. It was a good, long prayer about everything and everybody. Instead of listening, Tom watched a fly that had lit on the back of the pew in front of him. Tom's hand itched to grab for it, but he waited until the closing sentence of the prayer. Then, the instant that he heard "Amen," Tom caught the fly, but Aunt Polly saw him and made him let the fly go.

The minister started his sermon. For a while, Tom listened, but soon the words were lost to him, although he was interested in the part that had to do with the taming of a lion—if they would let him do it.

The sermon continued—and Tom suffered. Presently he remembered a treasure he had, and got it out. It was a large black beetle, a "pinchbug," in a little box. When Tom took it out, the first thing the beetle did was to take him by the finger and bite him. Tom dropped the beetle and put his hurt finger into his mouth.

The beetle lay in the aisle, on its back, working its helpless legs, unable to turn over. Tom wanted to get it, but it was out of his reach. Other people, tired of the sermon, started to watch the beetle too.

Soon a poodle dog who had wandered into the church came idling down the aisle. He saw the beetle, surveyed it, and sniffed at it. Then he began to play with it by snatching at it and pushing it between his paws. At last he grew tired of the play—and careless, for he got his chin too close to the beetle—the pinchbug bit him.

There was a sharp yelp. The poodle jerked its head and the beetle fell a couple of yards away and lit on its back once more. The people watching shook with a gentle inward joy. Tom was entirely happy.

But the dog looked foolish. He wanted revenge. He went to the beetle and began to attack it. The dog jumped at it, snatched at it with his teeth. But, he grew tired once more, after a while, and for a change chased a fly and followed an ant around until he forgot the beetle entirely—and sat down on it!

Then there was a wild yelp of agony and the poodle

went sailing up the aisle. The dog crossed the church in front of the altar and flew down the other aisle. Then he crossed before the doors. He clamored up the first aisle again. At last the dog found his master and sprang into the master's lap. The man flung the dog out of the window, and the yelps quickly thinned away and died in the distance.

By this time the whole church was laughing. The sermon had come to a dead standstill. But soon the service continued, although the people couldn't help laughing, from time to time. At last church was over.

Tom Sawyer went home from church quite cheerful. He thought to himself that there was some satisfaction about divine service when there was a bit of variety in it. One thing, though, spoiled his thought. He was willing that the dog play with his pinchbug, but he didn't think it right that the dog had run off with it.

Tom Meets Becky Thatcher

Monday morning, the day that began another week of school, found Tom miserable. He lay thinking. Soon he wished that he were sick. Then he could stay home from school.

He began to think of excuses. He tried to find a stomachache, but he couldn't. He thought further. Suddenly he found something—one of his upper front teeth was loose. He was about to begin to groan, as a starter, when he remembered that his aunt would pull the tooth —and that would hurt. He decided to hold back the tooth for the present.

He thought further. For a while he could think of nothing. Then he remembered hearing the doctor tell about a thing that laid up a patient for two or three weeks and almost caused the loss of a finger. He looked at his own sore toe. He didn't know the signs of the sickness, but, he decided to take a chance.

Tom started to groan. Sid slept on. Tom groaned louder, and actually thought that he began to feel pain in the toe. But there was no result from Sid.

Tom was panting with his work, by this time. He took a rest, then gave several good groans. But Sid snored on.

Tom became annoyed. He said, "Sid, Sid!" and shook him. This worked—Sid yawned, stretched, sat up with a snort, and began to stare at Tom. Tom went on groaning.

Sid said, "Tom, Tom! What's the matter?" He looked at Tom anxiously and shook him.

Tom moaned out, "Oh, don't, Sid! Don't shake me!"

"Why, what's the matter, Tom? I'll call auntie."

"No, never mind—it'll be over by and by, maybe."

"But don't groan so, Tom, it's awful! How long you been this way?"

"Hours. Ouch! Oh, don't stir so, Sid, you'll kill me!"

"Tom, why didn't you wake me sooner? Oh, Tom, *don't*! What *is* the matter?"

"I forgive you everything, Sid." Tom groaned. "—Everything you've ever done to me. When I'm gone—"

"Oh, Tom, you aren't dying, are you? Don't, Tom— oh, don't! Maybe—"

"I forgive everybody, Sid." Tom groaned again. "Tell 'em so, Sid. And Sid, you give my window sash and my cat with one eye to that new girl that's come to town, and tell her—"

But Sid had snatched his clothes and gone for help. Tom was suffering really now, so well was his mind working. His groans had a real sound.

Sid, downstairs, said, "Oh, Aunt Polly, come! Tom's dying!"

"Dying?"

"Yes'm. Don't wait—come quick!"

"Rubbage! I don't believe it!"

But she fled upstairs—with Sid and Mary at her heels. Her face grew white, too. When she reached the bedside, she gasped out:

"You, Tom! What's the matter with you?"

"Oh, auntie, I'm—"

"What's the matter with you—what *is* the matter, child?"

"Oh, auntie, my sore toe's dead!"

Aunt Polly sank into a chair, half laughing, half crying. Then she said, "Tom, what a scare you gave me. Now stop this and get out of bed."

The groans stopped. The pain vanished from the toe. Tom felt a little foolish. He said, "Aunt Polly, it *seemed* dead, and it hurt so I never minded my tooth at all."

"Your tooth? Indeed, what's the matter with your tooth?"

"One of them's loose, and it hurts perfectly awful!"

"There, there, now, don't groan. Open your mouth —well, your tooth *is* loose, but you're not going to die about that. Mary, get me a silk thread and a chunk of fire out of the kitchen."

Tom begged:

"Oh, please, auntie, don't pull it out! It doesn't hurt any more—I don't want to stay home from school!"

"Oh, you don't, do you? So all this was because you thought you'd get to stay home from school and go fishing? Tom, Tom—I love you so, but you seem to try every way you can to break my old heart with your tricks."

By this time everything was ready for the dentist. She tied one end of the silk thread to Tom's tooth with a loop. The other end she tied to the bedpost. Then she seized the chunk of fire and suddenly thrust it almost into the boy's face. The tooth was out.

As Tom went to school, he was the envy of every boy he met because the gap in his teeth let him spit in a new and different way. Quite a crowd of boys followed him to see him spit.

Shortly, on the way to school, Tom came upon Huckleberry Finn, son of the town drunkard and an

outcast like his father. Huckleberry didn't have to go to school, or to church. There was no one to make him go. He could sit up as late as he pleased. He was always the first boy to go barefoot in the spring and the last one to put on shoes in the fall. He never had to wash, nor put on clean clothes. His clothes were castoffs from men. His hat had a big chunk cut out of the brim. His coat, when he wore one, was always too big and hung nearly to his heels. One suspender held up his pants which dragged because the legs were too long.

Tom hailed him:

"Hello, Huckleberry!"

"Hello yourself—and see how you like it."

"What's that you got?"

"Dead cat."

"Let me see him, Huck. My, he's pretty stiff! Where'd you get him?"

"Bought him off a boy."

"What'd you give?"

"Blue ticket and a bladder I got at the butcher house."

"Where'd you get the blue ticket?"

"Ben Rogers two weeks ago for a hoop stick."

"Say—what are dead cats good for, Huck?"

"Good for? Cure warts with."

"No! Is that so? I know something that's better!"

"I bet you don't! What is it?"

"Why, spunk water."

"Spunk water! I wouldn't give a dern for spunk water!" Huck could swear wonderfully.

"You wouldn't, wouldn't you?! D'you ever try it?"

"No—but Bob Tanner did."

"Shucks! Tell me how Bob Tanner did it, Huck."

"Why, he took and dipped his hand in a rotten stump where rain water was."

"In the daytime?"

"Certainly."

"With his face to the stump?"

"Yes. At least, I think so."

"Did he *say* anything?"

"I don't think he did. I don't know."

"Aha! Talk about trying to cure warts with spunk water in such a way as that! You've got to do it right. You got to go all by yourself to the middle of the woods where you know there's a spunk water stump, and, just as it's midnight, you back up against the stump and jam your hand in and say:

'Barley-corn, Barley-corn, Indian-meal shorts,

Spunk water, spunk water, swallow these warts!'
and then walk away quick, eleven steps, with your eyes shut, and then turn around three times and walk home without speaking to anybody. If you speak, the charm's broken!"

"Well, that sounds like a good way. But, that's not the way Bob Tanner did it."

"No, sir, you can bet he didn't—he's got more warts than any boy in town! I've taken off thousands of warts from my hands that way, Huck. I play with toads so much I've always got lots of warts. Sometimes I take 'em off with a bean."

"Yeah, beans are good. I've done that."

"Have you? What's your way?"

"I split the bean, and cut the wart to get some blood. Then I put the blood on one piece of bean and bury the bean at midnight at the crossroads in the dark of the moon. Then I burn up the rest of the bean. You see, the piece that's got the blood on it will keep drawing and trying to get the other piece to it. That helps the blood to draw the wart, and, pretty soon, off she comes!"

"Yes, that's it, Huck, that's it! When you're burying it, though, if you say:

'Down, bean, off, wart—come no more to bother me!' it's better. But say—how do you cure 'em with dead cats?"

"Why, you take your cat and get in the graveyard about midnight when somebody that was wicked has been buried. When it's midnight a devil will come, or maybe two or three. You can't see 'em, only hear 'em, but, when they're taking the dead man away you heave your cat after 'em and say:

'Devil follow corpse, cat follow devil,
Warts follow cat, I'm done with you!'
That'll take off *any* wart!"

"Sounds right. D'you ever try it, Huck?"

"No, but old Mother Hopkins told me."

"Well, I guess it's so, then. They say she's a witch."

"Say! Why, Tom, I *know* she is! She witched my dad. Pop says so himself. He came along, one day, and saw her witching him, so he took up a rock. But, she dodged, or he'd have gotten her. Well, that very night he rolled off a shed where he was lying drunk and broke his arm."

"Why, that's awful. How did he know she was witching him?"

"Pop could tell, easy. When they keep looking at you, steady, they're witching you—especially if they mumble. Because when they mumble, they're saying the Lord's Prayer backwards."

"Say, Huck, when are you going to try the cat?"

"Tonight. I guess they'll come after old Hoss Williams tonight."

"But they buried him Saturday! Didn't they get him Saturday night?"

"Why, how you talk! How could their charms work, until midnight—and *then*, it's Sunday! Devils don't get around much on a Sunday, I guess."

"I never thought of that. That's so. Let me go with you?"

"Of course—if you aren't afraid."

"Afraid! 'Tisn't likely! Will you meow?"

"Yes—and you meow back, if you get a chance. Last time, you kept me meowing around until old Hays threw rocks at me and said, 'Dern that cat!' So I threw a brick through his window—but, don't you tell!"

"I won't. I couldn't meow that night, because auntie was watching me. But, I'll meow this time. Say—what's that?"

"Nothing but a tick."

"Where'd you get him?"

"Out in the woods."

"What'll you take for him?"

"I don't know. Don't want to sell him."

"All right. It's mighty small, anyway."

"I'm satisfied with it. It's good enough for me."

"Sure, there's ticks a-plenty. I could have a thousand of 'em if I wanted to."

"Well, why don't you? But this one is a pretty early tick, I guess. It's the first one I've seen this year."

"Say, Huck—I'll give you my tooth for him!"

"Let's see it."

Tom got out a bit of paper and carefully unrolled it. Huckleberry looked at it, longingly. At last he asked:

"Is it real?"

Tom lifted his lip and showed the hole.

"Well, all right," said Huckleberry, "it's a trade."

Tom put the tick in the same box that had lately held the pinchbug. The boys separated, each feeling richer than before.

When Tom reached the schoolhouse, he walked in with the manner of one who had come as fast as he could. He hung his hat on a peg and flung himself into his seat. But the teacher called out:

"Thomas Sawyer!"

Tom knew that when his name was called in full it meant trouble. He answered:

"Sir!"

"Come up here. Now, sir, why are you late *again,* as usual?"

Tom was about to lie, when he saw the new girl with two long tails of yellow hair hanging down a back that he knew by the electric feeling of love, and, next to her, *the only empty seat* on the girls' side of the schoolhouse! He said, at once:

"I STOPPED TO TALK WITH HUCKLEBERRY FINN!"

The teacher stared. The studying stopped. The pupils wondered if Tom had lost his mind. The teacher said:

"You—you did *what?!*"

"Stopped to talk with Huckleberry Finn."

"Thomas Sawyer, this is the most shocking thing

I've ever listened to! Take off your jacket!"

The teacher switched Tom until the teacher's arm was tired. Then he ordered:

"Now, sir, go and sit with the *girls*! And let this be a warning to you!"

The laughs that went around the room seemed to upset Tom, but what upset him most was the chance to be close to the girl of his dreams. He sat down next to her, but she slid away from him with a toss of her head. Nudges, winks, and whispers went through the room, but Tom sat still and seemed to study his book.

By and by the others stopped watching Tom, and the usual school murmur rose once more. Presently the boy began to steal secret glances at the girl. She saw them, made a face at him, and turned her back for the space of a minute.

When she carefully faced around again, a peach lay before her. She pushed it away. Tom gently put it back. She pushed it away again, but with less hatred. Tom returned it. Then she let it remain.

Tom wrote on his slate, "Please take it—I got more." The girl glanced at the words, but made no sign.

Tom began to draw on his slate, hiding his work with his left hand. For a time the girl wouldn't look at it, but curiosity began to show itself. The boy worked on as if he weren't thinking of her at all. At last she gave in, and whispered:

"Let me see it!"

Tom partly uncovered a drawing of a house with two roofs to it and smoke coming from the chimney. Then the girl became interested and she forgot everything else. When the picture was finished, she looked a moment, then whispered:

"It's nice—make a man."

The artist erected a man in the front yard who could have stepped over the house, but she was satisfied with the monster, and whispered:

"It's a beautiful man—now make a picture of me coming along."

Tom drew some curves with a full moon and straw limbs to it. He put a big fan in the fingers. The girl said:

"It's ever so nice—I wish I could draw!"

"It's easy," whispered Tom. "I'll teach you."

"Oh, will you? When?"

"At noon. Do you go home to dinner?"

"I'll stay, if you will."

"Good—I'll stay. What's your name?"

"Becky Thatcher. What's yours? Oh, I know—it's Thomas Sawyer."

"That's the name they use when they lick me. I'm Tom when I'm good. Call me Tom, will you?"

"Yes."

Now Tom began to write something on the slate, hiding the words from the girl. She begged to see. Tom said:

"Oh, it's nothing."

"Yes, it is."

"No it isn't. You don't want to see."

"Yes I do—indeed I do! Please let me."

"You'll tell."

"No, I won't—deed and deed and double deed, I won't!"

"You won't tell anybody at all? Ever, as long as you live?"

"No, I won't tell *any*body! Now let me see."

"Oh, *you* don't want to see!"

"Now that you treat me so, I *will* see!"

She put her small hand on his and pulled. Tom pretended to resist, but let his hand slip little by little until she saw these words:

"*I love you.*"

"Oh, you bad thing!" she exclaimed. She hit his hand a smart rap, but blushed, and looked pleased, nevertheless.

Just at this point Tom felt a grip on his ear and a

lifting. In that grip he was led across the room and put in his own seat. The whole school giggled. The teacher stood over him for a few awful moments, then moved away without saying a word. Although Tom's ear hurt, his heart was gay.

As the school quieted down, Tom tried to study, but the excitement within him was too great. He couldn't read. He mixed up his geography. He couldn't even spell little baby words.

7 Tom Engages
—And Disengages

The harder Tom tried to keep his mind on his book, the more his ideas wandered. So at last, with a sigh and a yawn, he gave it up.

It seemed to him that lunchtime would never come. The day was the sleepiest of sleepy days. Not a breath of air stirred. Away off, in the hot sun, the big hill baked in the heat. A few birds floated on lazy wing high in the sky. No other living thing could be seen but some cows, and they were asleep.

Tom wanted to be free, or to do something of interest. In his pocket, he found the box with the tick. He secretly took the box out and put the tick on his desk. He kept the tick from running off by turning him aside and back with a pin.

Next to Tom sat his good friend, Joe Harper. Joe had trouble trying to study, too, so he took a pin and helped move the tick. The fun grew. But soon Tom said that they were getting in each other's way. He put Joe's slate on the desk and drew a line down the middle of it from top to bottom.

"Now," said Tom, "as long as he's on your side, you can have him, but if he gets over on my side, I'll try to keep him."

"All right, go ahead. Start."

The tick moved from side to side with each boy trying his best to keep the insect on his side. It was fun until Joe kept the tick on his side most of the time. At last

Tom could stand it no longer. He reached over the line to get at the tick. Joe got angry:

"Tom, you let him alone!"

"I only want to stir him up a little, Joe."

"It isn't fair. You let him alone."

"Well, I'm not going to stir him much."

"Let him alone, I tell you!"

"I won't!"

"He's on my side of the line."

"Look here, Joe Harper, whose tick is it?"

"*I* don't care whose it is—he's on *my* side of the line and you can't touch him!"

"Well, I'll just bet I will, though. He's my tick and I'll do what I please with him!"

A big slap came down on Tom's shoulders, and another on Joe's. It was the schoolteacher. He had tiptoed over to the boys while they were busy with the tick. For two minutes the slaps continued while the whole school laughed.

When at last school broke up at noon, Tom flew to Becky Thatcher and whispered:

"Make believe you're going home. When you get to the corner, give the rest of 'em the slip, turn around, and come back. I'll go the other way and come back too!"

So Becky went off one way and Tom another. In a little while they came back to the school and had it all to themselves. They sat together, with a slate before them. Tom gave Becky his pencil and held her hand in his, guiding it, and so drew another house.

When they tired of art, the two talked. Tom was in heaven. He said:

"Do you love rats?"

"No! I hate them!"

"Well, I do. But I mean dead ones, to swing 'round your head with a string."

"No, I don't care for rats much. What *I* like is chewing gum."

"Oh, I should say so. I wish I had some now."

"Do you? I've got some. I'll let you chew it awhile, but you must give it back to me."

Tom agreed, so they chewed, turned about, and swung their legs against the bench in happiness.

"Were you ever at a circus?" said Tom.

"Yes, and my dad's going to take me again some time, if I'm good."

"I've been to the circus three or four times—lots of times. Church isn't anything to a circus—things are going on at a circus all the time! I'm going to be a clown when I grow up."

"Oh, are you! That will be nice. They're so lovely, all spotted up."

"Yes—and they get lots of money, Ben Rogers says. Say, Becky, were you ever engaged?"

"What's that?"

"Why, engaged to be married."

"No."

"Would you like to?"

"I guess so. I don't know. What is it like?"

"Like? Why, it's not like anything. You only just tell a boy you won't ever have anybody but him, ever, ever, *ever*! Then you kiss—and that's all. Anybody can do it."

"What do you kiss for?"

"Why, that, you know, is to—well, they always do that!"

"Everybody?"

"Why, yes—everybody that's in love with each other. Do you remember what I wrote on the slate?"

"Ye—yes."

"What was it?"

"I won't tell you!"

"Shall I tell *you*?"

"Ye—yes—but some other time."

"No, now!"

"No, not now—tomorrow."

"Oh, no, *now*! Please, Becky—I'll whisper it, ever so easy."

Becky hesitated. Tom slipped his arm around her waist and whispered the words softly. Then he added:

"Now you whisper it to me—just the same!"

She didn't want to, for a while, but then she said:

"Turn your face away so you can't see, and then I will. But you mustn't ever tell *any*body—*will* you, Tom? You won't, *will* you?"

"No, indeed, indeed I won't. Now, Becky!"

He turned his face away. She bent around until her breath stirred his curls, then, she whispered:

"I—love—you!"

Then she sprang away and ran around and around the desks and benches with Tom after her. At last she stopped in a corner and hid her face in her hands. Tom put his arm around her and begged:

"Now, Becky, it's all done—all over but the kiss. Don't be afraid of that—it isn't anything at all. Please, Becky!"

He pulled at her hands. By and by she gave up, and let her hands drop. Tom kissed her red lips and said:

"Now it's all done, Becky! And always after this, you know, you're never to love anybody but me, and you aren't ever to marry anybody but me, never, never, and forever! Will you?"

"No, I'll never love anybody but you, Tom, and I'll

never marry anybody but you—and you aren't to ever marry anybody but me, either!"

"Certainly! Of course. That's *part* of it. And always coming to school or going home you're to walk with me —when there isn't anybody looking. And you choose me and I choose you at parties, because that's the way you do when you're engaged."

"It's so nice! I never heard of it before."

"Oh, it's fun! Why, me and Amy Lawrence—"

Becky's eyes grew big and told Tom his mistake. He stopped, mixed up.

"Oh, Tom! Then I'm not the first you've ever been engaged to!"

She began to cry. Tom said:

"Oh, don't cry, Becky, I don't care for her any more!"

"Yes, you do, Tom—you know you do!"

Tom tried to put his arm around her, but she pushed him away and turned her face to the wall, and went on crying. Tom tried again, with soft words in his mouth, but he was pushed away again. Then his pride was up, and he went outside.

He stood around, outside, restless and uneasy. He looked at the door, every now and then, hoping she would come out to find him. But she didn't.

Then he began to feel bad and fear that he was in the wrong. He went back in. She was still standing in the corner, sobbing, with her face to the wall. Tom stood a moment, now knowing exactly what to do, then he said:

"Becky, I—I don't care for anybody but you!"

There was no reply, only sobs.

"Becky, please! Becky, won't you say something?"

More sobs.

Tom took out his most prized possession, a brass knob, and held it so that she could see it, and said:

"Please, Becky, won't you take it?"

She struck it to the floor. Then Tom marched out of the schoolhouse and over the hills and far away, to return to school no more that day.

Presently Becky began to suspect. She ran to the door. Tom was not in sight. She flew around to the playground. He wasn't there. She called:

"Tom! Come back, Tom!"

She listened. There was no answer, only silence, and loneliness. So she sat down to cry again and blame herself.

By this time the pupils began to gather again and she had to hide her grief and still her broken heart. There was no one among the strangers for the rest of the long, dreary afternoon to tell her troubles to.

8 A Pirate Enters
—But Robin Hood Leaves

Tom dodged through the streets until he was out of the way of the students who were going back to school, then he ran. Half an hour later he was on top of the big hill, and the schoolhouse could hardly be seen. He went into a big woods and sat down in the center of it.

Tom was sad. He sat long with his elbows on his knees and his chin in his hands, thinking. It seemed to him that life was but a trouble, at best. It must be peaceful, he thought, to be dead and dream forever and ever.

He thought about Becky. What had he done? Nothing! He had meant the best in the world, but he had been treated like a dog—like a very dog! She would be sorry some day—maybe when it was too late. Ah, if he could only die for a time!

What if he went away—ever so far away, beyond the seas—and never came back any more? How would she feel then? He would be a clown—no, he didn't feel like being funny. No, he would be a soldier, and return after long years, a hero. No—better still, he would join the Indians, hunt buffaloes, go on the warpath, and away in the future come back a great chief.

But no, there was something better even than this —he would be a pirate! That was it! He would sail the seas with his low, black ship, pistols in his belt and a cutlass at his side. He would unfurl his black flag with the skull and crossbones on it—and make people shudder! His name would fill the world, and everyone would whisper, "It's Tom Sawyer, the Pirate!—the Black Avenger of the Spanish Main!"

Yes, it was settled. He would be a pirate. He would run away from home and enter upon it. He would start the very next morning. But he must begin to get ready now.

Tom went to a rotten log near him and began to dig under one end of it with his jackknife. He soon struck wood that sounded hollow. He put his hand there and uttered this charm:

"What hasn't come here, *come*! What's here, *stay* here!"

Then he scraped away the dirt and uncovered a little box made of shingles. In it lay a marble. Tom was puzzled. He scratched his head and said:

"Well, that beats anything!"

Then he tossed the marble away and stood thinking. The truth was, he had buried the box with the marble here before. But, if you buried a marble in the woods and said certain words and left the marble there for two weeks, all the marbles you had ever lost would gather themselves there. Tom had buried marbles before, but he had never been able to find the places he had hid them!

He puzzled over the matter some time. Finally he decided that some witch had broken the charm. He thought he would make sure about that so he looked around until he found a small sandy spot with a little hole in it. He laid himself down, put his mouth close to the hole, and called:

"Doodlebug, doodlebug, tell me what I want to
    know!

Doodlebug, doodlebug, tell me what I want to
    know!"

The sand moved. Presently a small black bug appeared for a second, then darted into the sand again.

"He can't tell. It *was* a witch that did it. I knew it!"

Tom knew that you can't fight witches, so he gave up trying to work the charm. He looked for the marble he had thrown away but he couldn't find it. He went back to the exact spot he had tossed the marble away. Then he took another marble from his pocket, tossed it in the same way, and said:

"Brother, go find your brother!"

He watched where it stopped, went there, and looked. He couldn't find it, so he tried two more marbles. The last one was successful. He found two.

Just here the sound of a toy tin trumpet came through the green forest. Tom threw off his jacket, rolled up his trousers, raked away some brush behind the rotten log where a rude bow and arrow, a lath sword, and a tin trumpet were hidden, and in a moment had seized these things and bounded away, barelegged, with a fluttering shirt. He stopped under a great elm, blew an answering blast, and commanded a make-believe company:

"Hold, my merry men! Keep hid till I blow!"

Now appeared Joe Harper, dressed, and with a sword, like Tom. Tom called:

"Hold! Who comes here into Sherwood Forest without my pass?"

"Guy of Guisborne wants no man's pass! Who art thou that—that—"

"Dares to hold such language," said Tom, helping, for the boys talked the Robin Hood story, from the book, from memory.

"Who art thou that dares to hold such language?"

"I? Indeed! I am Robin Hood, as thy caitiff carcass soon shall know!"

"Then art thou, indeed, that famous outlaw? Right gladly will I dispute with thee the passes of the merry wood. Have at thee!"

They took their wooden swords, made a fencing position, foot to foot, and began a serious, careful fight, two steps up and two steps back. By and by Tom shouted:

"Fall! Fall! Why don't you fall?"

"I won't! Why don't you fall yourself? You're getting the worst of it!"

"Why, that isn't anything. *I* can't fall! That isn't the way it's in the book—the book says, 'Then, with one backhanded stroke, he slew poor Guy of Guisborne.' So turn around and let me hit you in the back."

There was no arguing with the book, so Joe turned, got the stroke of a sword, and fell.

"Now," said Joe, getting up, "you've got to let me kill *you*. That's fair."

"Why, I can't do that, it's not in the book!"

"Well, it's blamed mean—that's all."

"Well, say, Joe, you can be Friar Tuck, or Much, the miller's son, and slam me with a quarter staff. Or I'll be the Sheriff of Nottingham and you be Robin Hood a little while and kill me."

This was done. Then Tom became Robin Hood again, until, at last, Robin Hood was burned under the greenwood tree where the arrow fell. But Tom lay on a thorn and sprang up too quickly to be a good dead Robin Hood.

At last the boys hid their outfits and went home, grieving that there were no outlaws any more. They said they would rather be outlaws a year in Sherwood Forest than President of the United States forever.

9 Grave Events Open in the Graveyard

At half past nine, that night, Tom and Sid were sent to bed, as usual. They said their prayers, and Sid was soon asleep. Tom lay awake, and waited.

The clock struck ten. He would have tossed in bed, but he was afraid he might wake Sid. He lay still and stared into the dark. Everything was still, so still that the ticking of the clock was very loud. Old beams began to crack. The stairs creaked. He heard Aunt Polly snoring. A dog howled.

Tom was in an agony, waiting. At last he was sure that time had stopped. He began to doze. The clock chimed eleven, but he did not hear it. Then there came in his dreams, it seemed, the meowing of a cat.

The raising of a neighboring window disturbed him. A cry of "Scat!" and the crash of an empty bottle against the back of his aunt's woodshed brought him wide awake. A minute later he was dressed, out of the window, and creeping along the roof joining the woodshed. He meowed carefully, once or twice, as he went.

From the woodshed roof he jumped to the ground. Huckleberry Finn was there, with his dead cat. The boys moved off and disappeared into the dark.

At the end of half an hour they were in the graveyard. It was on a hill, about a mile and a half from town. It was an old graveyard with sunken graves and a crazy, crooked, old board fence around it. Tall grass and weeds were everywhere.

A faint wind moaned through the trees. Tom

feared it might be the spirits of the dead, complaining of being disturbed. The boys talked little, only whispered, for they were scared. They found the new grave they were seeking and sheltered themselves under three great elms near it.

They waited in silence for what seemed a long time. An owl hooted. Everything else was dead stillness. Tom couldn't bear the silence any longer, he had to talk, so he said in a whisper:

"Hucky, do you believe the dead people like it for us to be here?"

Huckleberry whispered:

"I wish I knew. It's awful sacred like, *isn't* it?"

"You bet it is!"

There was a long pause while the boys thought about this matter. Then Tom whispered:

"Say, Hucky—do you think Hoss Williams hears us talking?"

"Of course he does! At least, his spirit does."

Tom was alarmed. After a pause he said:

"I wish I'd said *Mister* Williams! But I never meant any harm. Everybody calls him Hoss."

"A body can't be too particular how he talks about these here dead people, Tom," Huck warned.

The conversation died again. Presently Tom seized Huck's arm and said:

"Sh-h-h!"

"What is it, Tom?" The two grabbed each other with beating hearts.

"Sh-h-h! There 'tis again! Didn't you hear it?"

"I—"

"There! Now you hear it."

"Lord, Tom, they're coming! They're coming, sure. What'll we do?"

"I don't know. Think they'll see us?"

"Oh, Tom, they can see in the dark, same as cats! I wish I hadn't come!"

"Oh, don't be afraid. *I* don't believe they'll bother us. We aren't doing any harm. If we keep perfectly still, maybe they won't notice us at all."

"I'll try to, Tom, but Lord, I'm afraid!"

"Listen!"

The boys bent their heads together and scarcely breathed. A sound of low voices floated up from the far end of the graveyard.

"Look! See, there!" whispered Tom. "What is it?"

"It's devil fire! Oh, Tom, this is awful!"

Some dim figures approached through the dark, swinging a lantern that threw streaks of light on the ground. Huckleberry whispered, with a shudder:

"It's the devils, sure enough! Three of 'em! Lordy, Tom, we're goners! Can you pray?"

"I'll try, but don't you be afraid—they aren't going to hurt us! Now I lay me down to sleep, I—"

"Sh-h-h!"

"What is it, Huck?"

"They're *humans*! One of 'em is, anyway. One of 'em's old Muff Potter's voice!"

"No, it can't be. Is it?"

"I bet I know it is. Don't you stir nor budge. He won't notice us. He's drunk, likely, the same as usual."

"All right. Here they come again! Say, Huck, I know another of those voices; it's Injun Joe!"

"That's so! I'd rather they were devils. What can they be up to?"

The whispering stopped, for the three men had reached the grave of Hoss Williams and stood within a few feet of the boys' hiding place.

"Here it is!" said the third man. He held the lantern up and showed the face to be young Dr. Robinson.

Potter and Injun Joe were carrying a wheelbarrow with a rope and a couple of shovels on it. They put down their load and began to dig open the grave. The doctor put the lantern at the head of the grave and came and sat down with his back against one of the elm trees. He was so close the boys could have touched him.

"Hurry, men!" he said in a low voice, "the moon might come out at any moment!"

They growled an answer and went on digging. For a time there was no noise except the digging, then a scraping. At last the coffin was brought up, torn open, and the body dumped out. The moon drifted from behind the clouds and showed the white face. The men put the body in the barrow, covered it with a blanket, and tied it down with the rope. Potter then said:

"Now it's ready, Sawbones, and you'll just out with another five, or here it stays!"

That's the talk!" said Injun Joe.

"Look here, what does this mean?" asked the doctor. "You required your pay in advance, and I've paid you."

"Yes, and you did more than that!" said Injun Joe, approaching the doctor, who jumped up. "Five years ago your father had me put in jail after you told him I wasn't at your house for any good the night I came to your house to ask for something to eat. Did you think I'd forget? I've *got* you, now, and you've got to *settle*, you know!"

He threatened the doctor with his fist. The doctor struck out suddenly and knocked him to the ground. Potter exclaimed:

"Here, now, don't you hit my friend!"

The next moment Potter was fighting with the doctor. The two struggled with might and main. Injun Joe sprang to his feet, picked up a long knife Potter had dropped after cutting the rope, and went creeping like a cat round and round the fighters.

All at once the doctor flung himself free, seized a heavy board from the ground, and knocked Potter down. The same instant Injun Joe saw his chance and

drove the knife to the end of the blade into the doctor's chest.

The doctor swayed and fell, partly upon Potter, flooding him with his blood. At this same moment the clouds blotted out the moon and this dreadful scene, and the two boys went speeding away in the dark.

Presently, when the moon came out again, Injun Joe was standing over Potter and the doctor. The doctor murmured something that couldn't be understood, then gave a long gasp or two, and was still. Injun Joe muttered:

"That's settled!"

Then he robbed the doctor's body. After that he put the knife in Potter's hand, and sat down on the broken coffin. Three—four—five minutes passed, then Potter began to stir and moan. He felt the knife in his hand, raised it, looked at it, and let it fall with a shudder. Potter sat up, pushing the doctor's body from him, gazed at it, and then around him, mixed up.

"Lord, Joe, how is this?" he asked.

"It's a dirty business," said Joe, without moving. "What did you do it for?"

"I! I never did it!"

"Look here! That kind of talk won't wash."

Potter trembled and grew white.

"I had no business drinking tonight. But it's in my head yet. I'm all in a muddle—can't remember, hardly. Tell me, Joe—*honest*, now, did I do it? I never meant to! Tell me how it was, Joe."

"Why, you two were fighting, and he hit you one with a board and you fell flat. Then, up you come, reeling and staggering, and you picked up the knife and jammed it into him just as he hit you another clip. And here you've laid, till now."

"Oh, I didn't know what I was doing! It was all on account of the whiskey, and the excitement, I think. I've never used a knife to fight with in my life, Joe! Joe, don't tell! Say you won't tell, Joe. You *won't* tell, *will* you, Joe?"

Potter dropped on his knees before the real murderer and clasped his hands, begging.

"No, you've always been fair and square with me, Muff Potter. I won't go back on you."

"Joe, you're an angel! I'll bless you for this the longest day I live!"

Potter began to cry. Injun Joe said, "Come, now, that's enough of that! You go off that way, and I'll go this. Move, now, and don't leave any tracks behind you!"

Potter started on a trot that quickly increased to a run. Injun Joe stood looking after him for a while, then muttered to himself:

"If he's as much stunned by the fighting and the whiskey as he looked, he won't think of the knife till he's gone so far he'll be afraid to come back after it— chicken-heart!"

Two or three minutes later the murdered doctor, the broken coffin, the open grave, and the body in the wheelbarrow under the blanket were seen by no one but the moon. All was quiet and still again.

10 The Night Ends Many Things

The two boys flew on and on, toward the village, speechless with horror. They glanced backward from time to time in fright, afraid they might be followed. Every stump seemed an enemy, and made them catch their breath.

"If we can only get to the old tannery before we break down!" panted Tom, in short catches between breaths. "I can't stand it much longer."

Huckleberry's hard breathing was his only reply. The boys fixed their eyes on the goal of their hopes and at last burst into the protecting shelter of the tannery. By and by their hearts slowed down, and Tom whispered:

"Huckleberry, what do you think'll come of this?"

"If Dr. Robinson dies, I guess hanging'll come of it."

Tom thought a while, then he said:

"Who'll tell? We?"

"What are you talking about? Suppose something happened and Injun Joe *didn't* hang? Why, he'd kill us some time or other, just as dead sure as we're here!"

"That's just what I was thinking to myself, Huck.

"If anybody tells, let Muff Potter do it, if he's fool enough. He's generally drunk enough."

Tom said nothing—went on thinking. At last he whispered:

"Huck, Muff Potter doesn't *know* it! How can he tell?"

"What's the reason he doesn't know it?"

"Because he'd just got that whack when Injun Joe did it. Do you think he could see anything, or know anything?"

"By hokey, that's so, Tom!"

"And besides, look-a-here—maybe that whack killed *him!*"

"No, it isn't likely, Tom. He had liquor in him, and when my pop is like that, nothing hurts him. He says so, himself. But if a man were sober—I don't know."

After another thinking pause, Tom said:

"Hucky, you sure you can keep mum?"

"Tom, we *got* to keep mum. *You* know that. That Injun Joe would drown us like a couple of cats if we were to tell. Tom, we *got* to swear to keep mum!"

"I'm agreed. Let's shake hands and swear."

"Oh, no, that wouldn't do for this! Shaking hands is for little things. A big thing like this ought to be in writing—in blood!"

Tom agreed. The idea was deep, dark, awful. He found a thin piece of board that lay in the moonlight, took a little piece of chalk out of his pocket, got the moon on his work to see by, and wrote these lines:

"Huck Finn and Tom Sawyer Swears they will keep mum about this and they wish they may Drop dead in their tracks if they ever tell and Rot."

Huck thought it wonderful that Tom could write with such words. He at once took a pin from his coat and was going to stick himself, but Tom said:

"Hold on! Don't do that. A pin's brass—it might have verdigrease on it!"

"What's 'verdigrease'?"

"It's poison, that's what it is. You just swallow some of it once—you'll see!"

Tom brought out one of his needles. Each boy pricked his thumb and squeezed out a drop of blood. Tom signed his initials, using his little finger for a pen, then he helped Huckleberry make an H and an F. The oath was complete. They buried the agreement close to the wall, saying secret words.

A figure crept secretly through a hole in the other end of the ruined building, now, but the boys did not notice it.

"Tom," whispered Huckleberry, "does this keep us from *ever* telling—*always?*"

"Of course it does. It doesn't make any difference *what* happens, we got to keep mum. We'd drop down dead—don't *you* know that?"

"Yes, I guess that's so."

They continued to whisper for some little time. Suddenly a dog set up a long, sad howl just outside, within ten feet of them. The boys grabbed each other in fright.

"Which of us does he mean?" gasped Huckleberry.

"I don't know—peep through the crack. Quick!"

"No! *You*, Tom!"

"I can't—I can't *do* it, Huck!"

"Please, Tom! There it is again!"

"Oh, lordy, I'm thankful!" whispered Tom. "I know that dog's voice. It's Bull Harbison's."

"Oh, that's good! I tell you, Tom, I was almost scared to death. I'd 'a' bet anything it was a *stray* dog."

The dog howled again. The boys' hearts sank.

"Oh, my! That isn't Bull Harbison's!" whispered Huckleberry. "Look, Tom!"

Tom, shaking with fear, put his eye to the crack. His whisper could hardly be heard as he said:

"Oh, Huck, it *is* a stray dog!"

"Quick, Tom, quick! Who does he mean?"

"Huck, he must mean us both—we're together!"

"Oh, Tom. I guess we're goners. I guess I know where *I'll* go. I've been so wicked."

"This comes of playing hookey and doing everything a fellow's told *not* to do. I might 'a' been good, like Sid, but no. If I ever get off this time, I'll go to Sunday School regular!" Tom began to sniffle a little.

"*You* bad!" said Huckleberry. He began to sniffle, too. "Alongside of me, Tom, you're pie. Oh, lordy, lordy, lordy! I wish I only had half your chance!"

Tom choked off and whispered:

"Look, Hucky, look! He's got his *back* to us!"

Hucky looked, with joy in his heart.

"Well, he has, by jingoes! Did he, before?"

"Yes, he did. But I never thought. Oh, this is bully! *Now* whom can he mean?"

The howling stopped. Tom's ears heard something else.

"Sh-h-h! What's that?" he whispered.

"Sounds like—like hogs grunting. No—it's somebody snoring, Tom!"

"That *is* it! Where is it, Huck?"

"I believe it's down the other end. Sounds so, anyway. Pop used to sleep there, sometimes, but I guess he isn't ever coming back to this town any more."

"Hucky, would you go, if I lead?"

"I don't like to, much. Tom, suppose it's Injun Joe!"

Tom lost courage. But soon the boys agreed to try. They tiptoed down, one behind the other. When they got within five steps of the snorer, Tom stepped on a stick, and it broke with a sharp snap. The snorer moaned, twisted a little, and turned his face into the moonlight. It was Muff Potter.

The boys' fears passed away, now. They tiptoed out. Outside the tannery, the long, sad howl rose on the night air again! They turned and saw the strange dog facing Potter, with the dog's nose pointing to heaven.

"Oh, geeminy, it's *him!*" exclaimed both boys, in the same breath.

"Muff Potter's a goner, Huck!" Tom declared.

The boys separated. When Tom crept in his bedroom window, the night was almost gone. He undressed carefully and fell asleep thinking nobody knew where he'd been. But Sid was awake, and had been so for an hour.

When Tom awoke, Sid was dressed, and gone. It looked late—why hadn't he been called? Within five minutes he was dressed and downstairs.

The family was still at table, but all had finished breakfast. No one scolded him. In fact, no one spoke. Tom sat down and tried to seem gay, but there was no answer, only silence. Tom's heart sank.

After breakfast, Aunt Polly took Tom aside. She wept over him and asked him how he could go and break her old heart so. Finally she told him to go ahead and ruin himself and bring her gray hairs with sorrow to the grave, for it was no use for her to try any more.

This was worse than a thousand whippings, and Tom's heart hurt as much as his tired body. He cried and begged for forgiveness. He promised over and over again to reform. Then Aunt Polly let him go, but Tom felt she hadn't completely forgiven him.

Tom felt unhappy. He didn't even care to get revenge on Sid. He went to school gloomy and sad and took his punishment, along with Joe Harper, for playing hookey the day before.

Then he took his seat, put his elbows on the desk, and rested his chin in his hands. He stared at the wall with a suffering that has reached the limit and can go no further.

His elbow was pressing against something hard on his desk. After a long time he slowly changed his position and looked. It was an object in a paper. He unrolled it. It was his brass knob!

Tom gave a big, long, lingering sigh, and his heart broke. This was the final straw that broke the camel's back.

11 *Muff Potter Goes to Jail*

Near noon the whole village was suddenly shocked with the horrible news of the murder in the graveyard. Everyone heard the story. The teacher gave holiday for that afternoon and closed the school.

A bloody knife had been found close to the murdered doctor. The knife had been recognized by somebody as belonging to Muff Potter. Another person said that he had come upon Potter washing himself in the river and that Potter had sneaked off about one or two o'clock in the morning. The town had been searched for him, but he could not be found. The sheriff and his men were looking for him.

All the town was going to the graveyard. Tom forgot about his heartbreak. He joined the crowd. He really didn't want to go, but something drew him on.

At the dreadful place Tom squeezed through the crowd and saw the sight again. It seemed years since last night. Somebody pinched his arm. He turned, and his eyes met Huckleberry's. Then both looked away so no one would notice their glances. But everybody was talking about the murder:

"Poor fellow!" "Poor young fellow!" "This ought to be a lesson to graverobbers." "Muff Potter will hang for this if they catch him!" "It was a judgment. God's hand is here!"

Now Tom shivered from head to heel—he saw Injun Joe! At this moment the crowd began to move, and voices shouted, "There he is! He's coming himself!"

"Who? Who?" twenty voices asked.

"Muff Potter!"

"He's stopped! Look out, he's turning—don't let him get away!"

But Muff Potter wasn't trying to get away—he only looked puzzled. But a person said:

"Look at him! He wanted to come and take a look at his work—but he didn't expect any company!"

The sheriff took Potter by the arm and brought him through the crowd. When Potter stood before the murdered man, he shook, put his face in his hands, and burst into tears.

"I didn't do it, friends!" he sobbed. "Upon my word I never!"

"Who said you did?" shouted a voice.

This seemed to carry home. Potter lifted his face and looked around sadly. He saw Injun Joe and exclaimed:

"Oh, Joe, you promised me you'd never—"

"Is that your knife?" demanded the sheriff.

Potter would have fainted if they had not caught him and eased him to the ground. Then he said:

"Something told me if I didn't come back and get—" He stopped. Then he waved his hand as if to give up and said, "Tell 'em Joe, tell 'em—it's no use, any more!"

Huck and Tom stood silent and stared at Injun Joe as he lied about what had happened. The boys expected every moment that God would send lightning down on Joe's head to stop his lying, but when he finished his story and still stood alive, they were sure Injun Joe had sold himself to the devil.

Somebody asked Muff Potter:

"Why didn't you run away? What did you want to come back here for?"

"I couldn't help it!" Potter moaned. "I wanted to, but I couldn't seem to go anywhere but here!" He fell to sobbing again.

Injun Joe told his story again, a few minutes later, to make it official. The boys were sure, now, that he belonged to the devil. They made up their minds to watch Joe, nights, whenever they could, so they could get a look at his master, the devil.

Injun Joe helped to put the body of the murdered doctor in a wagon to take it away. Some people in the crowd whispered that blood came from the body. The boys thought this would prove to the people who killed the doctor, but other people said:

"It was within three feet of Muff Potter when the blood came!"

Tom's terrible secret and his mind disturbed his sleep for as much as a week after this. One morning, at breakfast, Sid said:

"Tom, you roll around and talk in your sleep so much that you keep me awake half the time!"

Tom turned white and dropped his eyes.

"That's a bad sign," said Aunt Polly. "What have you got on your mind, Tom?"

"Nothing! Nothing I know of!" But Tom's hand shook so that he spilled his milk.

"And you do talk such stuff!" Sid added. "Last night you said, 'It's blood, it's blood, that's what it is!' You said that over and over. And then you said, 'I'll tell, I'll tell!' Tell *what*? What will you tell?"

Everything was swimming before Tom. He might have told what happened in the graveyard, but Aunt Polly said:

"It's that dreadful murder. I dream about it almost every night myself. Sometimes I dream that I did it!"

Mary said that she dreamed, too. Sid seemed satisfied, but Tom got out of the room as fast as he could.

After that, Tom decided not to take any chances. He complained of a toothache for a week, and tied up his jaw every night. He never knew that Sid listened every night, and often slipped the bandage off to hear better. Soon Tom's troublesome mind wore off. The toothache act grew bothersome and it was stopped. If Sid really made anything from Tom's sleep talking, he kept it to himself.

Tom didn't care for dead cats any more. When his schoolmates tried to find out the way a cat died, Tom stayed away. Sid noticed that and was surprised because it was more like Tom to take the lead in things like that. However, it wasn't long before inquests went out of style, and Tom wasn't bothered any more.

Every day or two during this time, Tom watched his chance and went to the jail window to give Muff Potter such small comforts as Tom could get hold of. The jail was a small brick building in a marsh at the edge of the village. No guards were there.

The people had a strong desire to tar and feather Injun Joe and chase him out of town for body stealing, but Joe was so dreaded nobody was willing to start the matter. He had been careful to tell of the fight, but not of the grave robbing. It was thought best not to try him in court, at present, so the matter was dropped.

12 Tom's Heart Mends
   —And Breaks, Again

One of the reasons Tom's mind drifted away from his secret troubles was that it had found a new and heavy one. Becky Thatcher had stopped coming to school!

At first Tom had struggled with his pride a few days and tried to forget her. He couldn't. He began to find himself hanging around Becky's house, nights, feeling very unhappy, for she was ill.

What if she should die! The thought disturbed him. He no longer took an interest in war, nor even pirates. The charm of life was gone. There was nothing but gloom left. He even put away his baseball bat.

Aunt Polly was worried. She began to try all kinds of remedies on him. She thought she was an expert for she bought all the "Health" books. She was always ready to try new pills or medicines. But not on herself, of course—she was never sick—but on her suffering neighbors.

The water treatment cure was new, now, and Tom's low condition was something she could try it on. She woke him at daylight every morning, took him to the woodshed, and poured buckets of cold water on him. Then she scrubbed him dry with a towel like a file, rolled him up in a wet sheet, and put him away under blankets to bring out the sickness.

Although she did this, Tom grew more and more pale and sad. She added hot baths, sitting baths, shower baths, and plunges. Tom remained as sad as ever. She fed him oatmeal and tried plasters. Every day she filled him up, with something.

Tom, by this time, didn't care what happened. This alarmed Aunt Polly—she made up her mind to wake him up, at any cost. She bought a lot of Pain-killer, a new medicine that was supposed to cure everything. She tasted it first—it burned her tongue—she knew it was good.

She gave Tom a teaspoonful and watched for the result. Her troubles were instantly at rest, her soul at peace again, for Tom woke up at once. In fact, one taste of the burny medicine and the boy could not have been more wild if she had built a fire under him.

Tom felt that it was time to wake up. It was all right to be sad with his broken heart over Becky, but the Pain-killer was too much. He thought over ways to get rid of the stuff and decided it was best to make believe he liked it. He asked for it often until Aunt Polly left the bottle with him.

But she watched the bottle secretly to see if Tom took any of the medicine. She found that the medicine really did go down, but, she didn't know that Tom was pouring it down a crack in the floor!

One day Tom was in the act of putting the Pain-killer in the floor crack when his aunt's yellow cat, Peter, came along. Peter eyed the teaspoon hungrily, purred, and begged for a taste. Tom said:

"Don't ask for it unless you want it, Peter!"

But Peter switched his tail that he did want it.

"You better make sure!"

Peter was sure.

"Now you've asked for it, I'll give it to you, because I'm not mean. But, if you find you don't like it, don't blame anybody but your own self!"

Peter was agreeable. Tom held his mouth open and poured down the Pain-killer. The cat sprang a couple of yards in the air, howled, and set off around and around the room upsetting the flowerpots. Next he rose on his hind feet, and howled again. Then he went tearing around the house again, knocking things down.

Aunt Polly entered in time to see him roll over twice, deliver a final yell, and sail through the open window, carrying the rest of the flowerpots with him. The old lady stood amazed, peering over her glasses. Tom lay on the floor, nearly dying with laughter. Aunt Polly asked:

"Tom, what on earth ails that cat?"

"*I* don't know, aunt," gasped the boy.

"Why, I never saw anything like it! What *did* make him act so?"

" 'Deed I don't know, Aunt Polly. Cats always act so when they're having a good time."

"They do, do they?"

But Aunt Polly looked around. Too late, Tom couldn't get the teaspoon sticking out from under the bed. She took it, held it up. Tom drew back, but Aunt Polly raised him by his ear and cracked his head soundly with her thimble.

"Now, sir, what did you want to treat that poor dumb beast so for?"

"I did it out of pity for him—because he hasn't any aunt!"

"Hasn't any aunt? What's that got to do with it?"

"Heaps—because if he'd had one, she would have burnt his stomach out of him without any more feeling than if he were human!"

Aunt Polly felt sorry. This was putting the thing in a new light—what was cruel to a cat *might* be cruel to a boy, too. Tears came to her eyes, and she put her hand on Tom's head and said gently:

"I was meaning for the best, Tom. And Tom, it *did* do you good."

Tom looked up in her face with a twinkle:

"I know you meant for the best, auntie—and so did I with Peter. It did *him* good, too—I never saw him get around so since—"

"Oh, go 'long with you, Tom! Now, try to see if you can't be a good boy, for once, and you needn't take any more medicine."

The next day Tom reached school ahead of time. As usual, of late, he hung about the schoolyard gate instead of playing with the boys. He was sick, he told them—and tried to seem to be looking everywhere but where he *was* looking—down the road for Becky.

Presently Jeff Thatcher came in sight, and Tom's face lighted. But when he saw that Jeff was alone, he turned sorrowfully away. When Jeff arrived, Tom tried to ask about Becky in a roundabout way, but Jeff said nothing about her.

Tom watched and watched, hoping every dress he saw would have Becky in it. At last dresses stopped coming. Tom stopped looking, entered the empty schoolhouse, and sat down to suffer.

Then one more dress passed in at the gate, and Tom's heart gave a great bound—it was Becky! The next instant he was outside, acting like an Indian, yelling, laughing, chasing boys, jumping over the fence, doing handsprings, standing on his head—all to get Becky to see him.

But Becky never looked. Tom came nearer, grabbing a boy's cap and throwing it on the school roof, war-whooping around, breaking through a group of boys and tumbling them in every direction, falling, at last, under Becky's nose, nearly knocking her down. But, she turned, with her nose in the air, and he heard her say:

"Humpf! Some people think they're mighty smart— always showing off!"

Tom's cheeks burned. He gathered himself up and sneaked off, crushed, his heart broken, again.

13 *Three Pirates Set Sail*

Tom's mind was made up now. He was gloomy and desperate. He was friendless, he said, and nobody loved him. When they found out what they had driven him to, they would be sorry. Yes, they had forced him to it at last. He would lead a life of crime. There was no choice.

By this time he was far down the road. The bell starting school tinkled faintly upon his ear. He sobbed, now, to think he should never, never hear that old sound any more. It was hard to be driven out into the cold world, he must go—but he forgave everybody.

Just at this point he met his old comrade, Joe Harper. Joe, too, looked hard-eyed and dismal. Tom was about to tell him that he was going into the great world never to return, but Joe had made up his mind to do the same thing and had come to hunt up Tom to tell him so. Joe had gotten a whipping for drinking cream he said he never even tasted. It was plain his mother was tired of him. There was nothing for him to do but go.

As the two boys walked sorrowing along, they agreed to stand by each other and be brothers and never separate till death ended their troubles. Then they began to plan. Joe was for living alone in a faraway cave, but after listening to Tom, he agreed a life of crime was better, and consented to be a pirate.

Three miles below the town where the big river was over a mile wide, there was a long, narrow island with wild woods and no people. That place, Jackson's Island, would be their port. Then they hunted up Huckleberry Finn, and he joined them at once. Shortly after, they parted, after agreeing to meet at a lonely spot on the riverbank two miles above the village at midnight. There was a small raft there which they meant to capture. Each agreed to bring as many supplies as he could steal—as became outlaws.

Before the afternoon was done, all had spread the fact that pretty soon the town would "hear something." Those who got this hint were told to "be mum and wait!"

About midnight Tom arrived with a boiled ham and a few little things and stopped in the bushes above the meeting place. The stars were shining. It was very still. Tom listened a moment, then gave a low whistle. It was answered in the same way. Then a low voice said:

"Who goes there?"

"Tom Sawyer, the Black Avenger of the Spanish Main. Name your names."

"Huck Finn, the Red-Handed, and Joe Harper, the Terror of the Seas."

" 'Tis well! Give the password!"

Two whispers gave the same awful word:

"BLOOD!"

Tom rolled his ham over the bluff and let himself down after it. He scratched himself, but under the bluff there was an easy path to the shore.

The Terror of the Seas had brought a side of bacon so big he was tired just getting it there. Finn, the Red-Handed, had stolen a frying pan and some tobacco. He also brought along a few corncobs to make pipes with.

The Black Avenger of the Spanish Main said that it would never do to start without some fire. That was a wise thought. Sitting around the fire, the pirates said

"Hist!" every now and then and "Let him have it!" if the enemy stirred because "Dead men tell no tales!"

They shoved off, presently, Tom in command, Huck at one oar and Joe at the other. Tom stood in the middle with folded arms and gave his orders in a low, stern whisper:

"Luff, and bring her to the wind!"

"Aye, aye, sir!"

"Steady, steady-y-y-y!"

"Steady it is, sir!"

"Let her go off a point!"

"Point it is, sir!"

"What sail's she carrying?"

"Courses, topsails, and flying jib, sir."

"Send the royals up! Lively, now!"

"Aye, aye, sir!"

"Hard a port! *Now*, men! Steady-y-y-y!"

"Steady it is, sir!"

The raft passed beyond the middle of the river. The boys pointed it right, and then rested on their oars. The river wasn't high and the current was soon moving the raft past the town. Two or three lights shone from the sleeping village. The Black Avenger wished "she" could see him now, as he was "looking his last." The other pirates were looking their last, too.

About two o'clock in the morning the raft grounded on the bar about two hundred yards above the head of the island. The boys waded back and forth until they had landed their supplies. They spread an old sail from the raft over a hollow in the bushes for a tent for the supplies, but they, themselves, decided to sleep in the open air in good weather, as became outlaws.

They built a fire against the side of a great log twenty or thirty steps in the dark forest, and then cooked some bacon in the frying pan, and used up half of the corn bread they had brought. It was glorious sport to be feasting in that wild, free way far from men —they said they would never return. The fire lit up their faces and threw shadows on the trees.

When the last slice of bacon was gone and the last of the bread eaten, the boys stretched themselves out on the grass, filled with contentment. Said Joe:

"*Isn't* it gay?"

"It's *nuts!*" declared Tom. "What would the boys say if they could see us now?"

"Say? Well, they'd just die to be here—hey, Hucky?"

"I guess so," said Huckleberry, "anyways, it suits *me!* I don't want anything better than this. I don't ever get enough to eat, generally—and here they can't pick on you!"

"It's just the life for me," said Tom. "You don't have to get up, mornings, and you don't have to go to school, and wash, and all that foolishness! You see, a pirate doesn't have to do *anything,* Joe, when he's ashore— but a hermit, that's different."

"Oh, yes, that's so," said Joe. "I'd a good deal rather be a pirate, now that I've tried it."

"You see," continued Tom, "people don't go much for hermits, nowadays, like they used to in old times. A hermit's got to sleep on the hardest place he can find, and put sackcloth and ashes on his head, and stand out in the rain, and—"

"What does he put sackcloth and ashes on his head for?" inquired Huck.

"*I* don't know—but he's *got* to do it. Hermits always do. You'd have to, if you were a hermit."

"Dern'd if I would!" said Huck.

"Well, what would you do?"

"I don't know. But, I wouldn't do that."

"Why, Huck, you'd *have* to! How'd you get around it?"

"Why, I just wouldn't stand it. I'd run away."

"Run away! Well, you *would* be a nice old slouch of a hermit—you'd be a disgrace!"

Huck did not answer—he was busy making a corn- cob pipe. Finished with the stem, he loaded the pipe with tobacco, lit it, and blew out clouds of smoke. Then Huck said:

"What do pirates have to do?"

Tom said:

"Oh, they just have a bully time—take ships and burn them, get the money and bury it on their islands, kill everybody in the ships—make 'em walk a plank."

"And they carry the women to the island," said Joe. "They don't kill the women."

"No," agreed Tom, "they don't kill the women—they're too noble. And the women are always beautiful, too."

"And don't they wear the bulliest clothes! Oh, no! All gold, silver, and diamonds!" added Joe.

"Who?" asked Huck.

"Why, the pirates!"

"Guess I'm not dressed for a pirate," said Huck, looking sadly at his own clothing. "I've none but these."

The other boys told him the fine clothes would come fast enough, later. They made him understand that his poor rags would do to begin with, though wealthy pirates started with the proper clothes.

Gradually their talk died out and sleep began to steal upon their eyelids. The pipe dropped from the fingers of the Red-Handed. He slept the sleep of the weary. The Terror of the Seas and the Black Avenger of the Spanish Main had trouble in getting to sleep. They said their prayers to themselves, but sleep wouldn't come, for they began to think they had been doing wrong to run away.

Next they thought of the stolen meat they had taken. They tried to tell themselves that they had taken apples scores of times. But conscience wasn't answered by such excuses—there was no getting around it that taking bacon and hams was plain, simple *stealing*—and there was a command against that in the Bible. They made up their minds they would not steal while in the pirate business.

At last these queer pirates, their minds at ease, fell peacefully to sleep.

14 The Pirates Find They Are Drowned

When Tom awoke in the morning, he wondered where he was. He sat up, rubbed his eyes, and looked around. Then he remembered.

It was cool gray dawn. Everything was peaceful and silent. Not a leaf stirred. A white layer of ashes covered the fire, but a thin blue breath of smoke still rose straight into the air. Joe and Huck still slept.

Far away in the woods a bird called. Another answered. Gradually the day grew lighter and Nature woke up as Tom watched. A green worm came along and crawled over him. He saw ants at work. A ladybug and tumblebug came next. The birds were getting noisy. Two squirrels came to look and a few butterflies fluttered along.

Tom stirred up the other pirates. They all raced away with a shout, and in a minute or two were undressed and in the shallow and warm water of the sand bar. The river had swept away the raft, but they didn't care.

They came back to camp clean, happy, and hungry, and soon had the campfire blazing again. Huck found a spring of clear cold water close by. While Joe was slicing bacon for breakfast, Tom and Huck stepped to the riverbank and began fishing. Almost at once they caught several fish. They fried the fish with the bacon. No fish had ever tasted so good before.

They lay around in the shade, after breakfast, then went off on an exploring expedition. They found the island was about three miles long and a quarter of a mile wide. At one place the island was only about two hundred yards from shore. There were great trees with grapevines hanging from them. Now and then there were spaces with grass filled with flowers.

They took a swim about every hour. It was the middle of the afternoon when they got back to camp. They were too hungry to stop to fish, but ate cold ham, and then threw themselves down in the shade to talk.

But the talk soon began to drag, and then died. The stillness began to make the boys lonely. They fell to thinking. Soon they were all homesick. Even Finn, the Red-Handed, was dreaming of his doorsteps and empty barrels—his home. But all were ashamed of their weakness, and none was brave enough to speak his thought.

For some time, now, the boys had been hearing a peculiar sound in the distance. They listened carefully. There was a long silence, then a deep "Boom!" came floating down.

"What is it?" exclaimed Joe, under his breath.

"I wonder!" said Tom, in a whisper.

"It isn't thunder," said Huckleberry, "because thunder—"

"Hark!" said Tom. "Listen—don't talk!"

They waited a time that seemed very long, and then the same "Boom!" broke the air.

"Let's go see!"

They sprang to their feet and hurried to the shore toward the town. They parted the bushes on the bank and looked out over the water. A little steamboat was about a mile below the village, drifting with the current, her broad deck crowded with people. A great many small boats were being rowed or floating with the stream near the steamboat, but the boys couldn't see what the men in them were doing. Again the boys heard the same dull sound.

"I know now!" exclaimed Tom. "Somebody's drowned!"

"That's it!" said Huck. "They did that last summer, when Bill Turner got drowned. They shoot a cannon over the water, and that makes him come to the top!"

"By jings, I wish I was over there, now!" said Joe.

"I do too," said Huck. "I'd give heaps to know who it is!"

The boys still listened and watched. Presently an idea flashed through Tom's mind, and he exclaimed:

"Boys! I know who's drowned—it's us!"

They felt like heroes in an instant. Here was a victory—they were missed, people were shedding tears for them, hearts were breaking on their account. Best of all, everyone was talking about them. This was fine. It was worthwhile to be a pirate, after all.

As twilight drew on, the steamboat went back to its business of carrying people across the river and the small boats disappeared. The pirates returned to camp. There was great joy over their fame and the trouble they were making. They caught fish, cooked supper, and ate it. Then they fell to guessing what the village was thinking and saying about them.

When the shadows of night closed in, they gradually stopped talking and sat gazing into the fire thinking of other things. Tom and Joe couldn't keep back thoughts of certain persons at home. Both grew troubled and unhappy. By and by Joe said he wondered how the others might look when they got back home—not right now, but—.

Tom shamed him by poking fun at him. Huck joined in with Tom, and Joe was glad to get out of it with as little mark of chicken-hearted homesickness as he did.

The night deepened. Huck began to nod, then snore. Joe followed next. Tom lay upon his elbows, watching the two. At last he got up carefully, on his knees, looked among the grass and found several pieces of thin white bark. Then he knelt by the fire and wrote something on each with his red chalk. One he rolled up and put in his jacket pocket. The other he put in Joe's hat, along with a lump of chalk, a rubber ball, three fishhooks, and a crystal marble.

Tom then tiptoed his way carefully among the trees. When he felt that he was out of hearing, he straightway broke into a run in the direction of the sand bar where the shore was nearest.

15 A Pirate Steals a Visit Home

A few minutes later Tom was in the water, wading toward the shore. By the time the water came up to his middle, he was halfway over. When the water became too deep for wading, he started to swim. He reached the shore, finally, and pulled himself on the bank.

Tom put his hand on his jacket pocket, found his piece of bark safe, and then started through the woods, following the shore, toward the village. Shortly before ten o'clock he came out into the open near the town and saw the steamboat next to the high bank. Everything was quiet under the stars. He crept down the bank, watching carefully, slipped into the water, swam three or four strokes, and climbed into the little boat tied to the end of the steamboat. He hid under the sides of the boat and waited, panting.

Presently the steamboat bell rang and a voice gave the order to "Cast off!" In a minute or two the little boat was being pulled by the steamboat across the river toward the village. Tom felt happy in his success, for he knew it was the boat's last trip for the night. In about fifteen minutes the steamboat slowed down. Tom slipped into the water and swam ashore below the landing so that no one could see him.

He flew along deserted alleys and shortly found himself at his aunt's back fence. He climbed over and looked in at the sitting room window, for a light was on there. There sat Aunt Polly, Sid, Mary, and Joe Harper's mother, talking.

Tom went to the door and began softly to lift the latch. Then he pressed gently, and the door opened a crack. Between the group and Tom was a couch. He squeezed through the door and under the couch just in time as Aunt Polly said:

"Why, the door's open, I believe. Why, of course it is. Sid, go along and shut it."

Tom, under the couch, could almost touch his aunt's foot. She continued:

"But as I was saying, he wasn't *bad,* so to say—just full of life, like a colt. *He* never meant any harm, and he was the best-hearted boy that ever was!" She began to cry.

"It was just so with my Joe," said Mrs. Harper, "—always full of the devil and up to every trick. But he was kind as could be—and bless me, to think I whipped him for taking that cream I later remembered I threw out because it was sour! And to think I'm never to see him again in this world, never, never, never!" Mrs. Harper sobbed as if her heart would break.

"I hope Tom's better off where he is," said Sid, "but, if he'd been better in *some* ways—"

"*Sid!*" Aunt Polly glared at him. "Not a word against my Tom, now that he's gone! Oh, Mrs. Harper, I don't know how to give him up. He was such a comfort to me."

She went on talking. Mrs. Harper found many more things to feel sorry about Joe for. Tom could hear Mary crying and putting in a kindly word for him from time to time. He felt like rushing out from under the couch and showing himself, but this was too much fun, so he lay still.

He went on listening and found out that everybody guessed that the boys had drowned while taking a swim or using the raft, since the raft was found five or six miles below the village. It was believed the boys had gone down in deep water, since their bodies could not be found. If the bodies continued missing until Sunday, all hope would be given up, and the funerals would be preached on that morning. Tom shuddered.

Mrs. Harper gave a sobbing good night and then had another good cry before she left. Aunt Polly was very tender to Sid and Mary as they went up to bed. Sid sniffled a bit and Mary went off crying with all her heart. Then Aunt Polly knelt down and prayed for Tom. Before she was through, Tom was crying, too, but he stayed under the couch until she went to bed.

At last, when Tom felt sure Aunt Polly was asleep, he stole out into her bedroom to look at her. His heart was full of pity for her. He took out his note of bark and placed it by the candle. But then he changed his mind and put the bark back in his pocket, bent over and kissed Aunt Polly, and quietly went out closing the door behind him.

Tom made his way back to the boat landing, found nobody there, untied the little boat from the steamship, slipped into it, and was soon rowing upstream and across the river. He soon landed on the other side. For a while he thought of capturing the boat, as a pirate should, but he knew they would look for it and maybe find the pirate camp. So he stepped ashore and entered the wood.

He sat down, took a long rest to keep awake, then started back to the camp. The night was nearly over before he found himself near the island. He waited until the sun was up, then swam across to the camp.

A little later he was close enough to the other pirates to hear Joe say:

"No, Tom's true-blue, Huck, and he'll come back. He won't desert. He knows that would be a disgrace to a pirate. Tom's too proud for that. He's up to something or other. I wonder what?"

"Well, these things are ours, anyway, aren't they?"

"Pretty near, but not yet, Huck. The writing says they are if he isn't back by breakfast."

"Which he is!" exclaimed Tom, stepping importantly into camp.

A wonderful breakfast of bacon and fish was soon made, and as the boys set to work upon it, Tom told about his trip. They were a proud company of heroes when the story was over. Then Tom hid himself in the shade to sleep till noon, while the other pirates got ready to fish and explore.

16 The Pirates Smoke the Peace Pipe

After dinner all the crew turned out to hunt for turtle eggs on the sand bar. They poked sticks into the sand, found a soft place, then dug with their hands. Sometimes they found fifty or sixty eggs in one hole. They had a famous fried egg feast that night, and another the next morning.

After breakfast they went swimming again out over the bar. They stood in the swift current which tripped their legs from under them from time to time to add to the fun. Now and then they splashed water in each other's faces, or ducked each other. When they were tired, they would run on the dry, hot sand, and lie there and cover themselves up with it, and by and by get into the water again. Finally they played circus.

Next they got their marbles and played every game they knew. Then Joe and Huck had another swim, but Tom didn't go because he had lost his good-luck charm made of rattlesnake rattles and he wanted to look for it. When he did find it, the other boys were tired of swimming and ready to rest.

They gradually wandered apart, dropped into the "dumps," and fell to looking up the river to where the village lay in the sun. Tom found himself writing "Becky" in the sand with his big toe. He scratched it out, and was angry with himself for his weakness. But he wrote it again—he couldn't help it.

Joe's spirits were very low. He was so homesick that he could hardly stand it. He was ready to cry. Huck was sad, too, and even Tom. Tom tried hard not to show it, and said, with a great show of cheerfulness:

"I bet there's been pirates on this island before, boys. They've hid treasures here, somewhere! We'll explore it again. How'd you like to light on a chest full of gold and silver—hey?"

But there was no answer. No one was interested any more. Tom tried one or two other tricks, but they failed, too. Joe sat poking up the sand with a stick and looking very gloomy. Finally he said:

"Oh, boys, let's give it up! I want to go home. It's so lonesome."

"Oh, no, Joe, you'll feel better by and by," said Tom. "Just think of the fishing that's here."

"I don't care for fishing. I want to go home!"

"But, Joe, there isn't such another swimming place anywhere!"

"Swimming's no good. I mean to go home."

"Oh, shucks, baby! You want to see your mother, I guess."

"Yes, I *do* want to see my mother—and you would, too, if you had one. I'm no more baby than you are!" Joe sniffled a little.

"Well, we'll let the crybaby go home to his mother, *won't* we, Huck? Poor thing—does it want to see its mother? And so it shall. *You* like it here, *don't* you, Huck? We'll stay, won't we?"

Huck said "Y-e-s"—but he didn't mean it.

"I'll never speak to you again as long as I live!" said Joe, rising. "There, now!" He moved away and began to get ready to go.

"Who cares!" declared Tom. "Nobody wants you to. Go 'long home and get laughed at. Oh, you're a nice pirate. Huck and I aren't crybabies. We'll stay, won't we, Huck? Let him go if he wants to. I guess we can get along without him, perhaps."

But Tom was uneasy, nevertheless, to see Joe getting ready to leave. Besides, Huck was watching Joe as if Huck wanted to go too. Presently, without a goodbye, Joe began to wade off toward the shore.

Tom's heart began to sink. He glanced at Huck. Huck could not bear the look, and dropped his eyes. Then Huck said:

"I want to go, too, Tom. It was getting so lonesome, anyway, and now it'll be worse. Let's go too, Tom."

"I won't! You can all go, if you want to. I mean to stay!"

"Tom, I better go."

"Well, go—who's stopping you?"

Huck began to pick up his things. He said:

"Tom, I wish you'd come, too. Now you think it over. We'll wait for you when we get to shore."

"Well, you'll wait a blamed long time, that's all!"

Huck started away. Tom stood looking after him with a strong desire to forget his pride and go too. He hoped the boys would stop and come back, but they waded slowly on. He knew nothing would stop them but the secret he had been holding back. He ran after them and yelled:

"Wait! Wait! I want to tell you something!"

They stopped and turned around. When Tom got to where they were, he told them his secret. At last, when they saw the point Tom was driving at, they set up a war whoop and said it was a good idea, and if he had told them at first, they wouldn't have started away.

The lads came happily back, talking all the time about Tom's big plan. They went back to their playing, and after a dainty egg and fish dinner, Tom said he wanted to learn to smoke. Joe said he'd like to try, too. So Huck made pipes and filled them.

The boys stretched themselves out on their elbows and began to smoke. The smoke had an unpleasant taste, and they gagged a little, but Tom said:

"Why, it's easy! If I had known *this* was all, I'd have learned long ago."

"So would I," said Joe. "It's just nothing."

"Why, many a time I've looked at people smoking and wished I could do that," said Tom. "But I never thought I could."

"I believe I could smoke this pipe all day," said Joe. "*I* don't feel sick."

"Neither do I," said Tom. "*I* could smoke it all day. But I bet you Jeff Thatcher couldn't."

"Jeff Thatcher! Why, he'd keel over just with two draws. Just let him try it once. *He'd* see!"

"I bet he would. And Johnny Miller—I wish I could see him tackle it once."

"Oh, don't *I!*" said Joe. "Why, I bet you he couldn't any more do this than nothing. Just one little snifter would get him!"

" 'Deed it would, Joe. Say—I wish the boys could see us now."

"So do I!"

So the talk ran on. But soon it began to slow a bit, but the spitting increased. Their tongues burned. Their mouths began to water so much that they couldn't help swallowing some of the tobacco juice. They began to feel like throwing up.

Both boys looked very pale and miserable, now. Joe's pipe dropped from his fingers. Tom's followed. Both were spitting wildly. Joe said feebly:

"I lost my knife—guess I better go find it."

"I'll help you!" Tom said trembling. "You go over that way, and I'll hunt around the spring. You needn't come, Huck—we can find it!"

Huck sat down again. He waited an hour. Then he found it lonesome, and went to find his comrades. They were wide apart in the woods, both very pale, both fast asleep. But something told him that if they had had any trouble from their smoking they had gotten rid of it.

They didn't talk much at supper that night. After the meal Huck filled his pipe and was going to prepare theirs, too, but they said no, they weren't feeling well—something they ate had disagreed with them.

About midnight Joe awoke and called the boys. There was something in the air that seemed something was coming. The boys grouped themselves around the fire, the air was hot and sticky. They sat still, watchful, waiting. Beyond the light of the fire everything was black darkness.

A flash of lightning suddenly lit up the leaves, then vanished. By and by another came, a little stronger. Then another. Next a faint moan came sighing through the branches of the trees. The boys felt a breeze on their cheeks.

Now a flash turned night into day and thunder went rolling and tumbling down the heavens. A sweep of chilly air passed by. Another fierce flash lit the sky and a crash followed that seemed to split the treetops right over the boys' heads. They clung together in terror. A few big raindrops fell pattering upon the leaves.

"Quick, boys! Go for the tent!" exclaimed Tom.

They sprang away, but not before another blast roared through the trees and one blinding flash after another came along with more sounds of thunder. And

now the rain poured down. However, one by one the boys at last got under the tent, cold, scared, and streaming with water.

The storm rose higher and higher, and presently the sail that made the tent went winging away on the wind. The boys seized each other's hands and fled to the shelter of a great oak that stood upon the riverbank.

Now the storm was at its highest. Lightning flashed everywhere. The wind drove the river into white foam, and every now and then a great tree fell crashing to the ground on the island. Thunder exploded everywhere until it seemed the storm would tear the island to pieces.

But at last the storm was done. The boys went back to their camp to find that the great tree that had served as their shelter was a ruin now, blasted by lightning. They were thankful they had not been under it when it happened.

Everything in camp was soaked, but the boys found a dry spot in a great log and at last had a fire burning again. They piled on great dead boughs till they had a roaring furnace and were glad-hearted once more. They had a boiled ham feast, and after that sat by the fire until morning, for there was not a dry spot to sleep on, anywhere.

They talked about their midnight adventure until the sun came up. Then they went out on the sand bar and lay down to sleep. After breakfast they felt rusty, and stiff-jointed, and a little homesick once more. Tom saw the signs and tried to cheer them up as well as he could, but they didn't care for the old games any more.

Tom reminded them of the great secret. That cheered them up for a while, and while it lasted, Tom said they ought to play Indian for a change. It wasn't long and they had war paint on their faces, were attacking an English settlement, and were killing and scalping each other by the thousands.

They assembled in camp toward supper time, hungry and happy. But now a difficulty arose—Indians smoked a pipe of peace. Two of the Indians almost wished they had remained pirates. However, there was no other way out, so with as much cheerfulness as they could show they called for the pipe and took their puff as it passed, in due form. And behold, they found that if they took a little whiff they didn't get sick enough to be uncomfortable. They were proud and happy to be Indians.

17 *Tom's Secret Comes Alive*

But there was no laughter in the little town that same afternoon. Joe's and Tom's families were dressing in black, with great grief and many tears. People in the village talked little, but they sighed often. The children could not enjoy the Saturday holiday, for they had no heart in their games and gradually gave them up.

In the afternoon Becky Thatcher found herself near the deserted schoolyard. She felt very sad. She said to herself, "Oh, if I only had a brass knob again! But I haven't anything now to remember him by." And she choked back a little sob.

"It was right here!" she went on. "Oh, if it were to do over again, I wouldn't say what I did for the whole world. But he's gone now. I'll never, never, never see him any more!" This thought broke her down, and she wandered away, with the tears rolling down her cheeks.

Then quite a group of boys and girls came by, stood looking over the school fences, and talked about the way Tom did this and Joe did that. Each one pointed out the exact spot the lost lads stood at the time. Then there was an argument about who saw the dead boys last. The group moved away, at last, still recalling memories of the lost heroes in hushed voices.

When Sunday School was finished, the next morning, the church bell began to toll, instead of ringing in the usual way. It was a very quiet Sunday, and the sad sound of the bell seemed in keeping with the hush that lay upon nature. The villagers began to gather, stopping a moment in the hall to talk in whispers about the sad event, but there was no whispering in the church— all was in silence, there. None could remember when the little church had been so full before.

There was finally a waiting pause and an unusual quiet. Then Aunt Polly entered, followed by Sid and Mary. The Harper family came in next. All were dressed in black. All the people and the old minister rose and stood until the mourners were seated in the front pew.

There was another silence, broken, at times, by muffled sobs. Then the minister spread his hands and prayed. A moving hymn was sung next. At last the minister began the funeral sermon.

The minister talked so nicely of the lost lads and their good points and bright futures that everyone there felt ashamed to think each had seen only the bad things in the poor boys. The preacher told stories from the lives of the missing to show the sweet, kind natures they really had. The people became more and more moved as the pitiful stories went on till at last the whole company broke down and joined in the sobs, even the preacher himself, who cried in the pulpit.

There was a movement in the gallery, which nobody noticed. A moment later the church door creaked open. The minister raised his streaming eyes above his handkerchief, and what he saw made him stand like a stone.

First one and then another pair of eyes followed the minister's. Then almost with one move all the people rose and stared while the three dead boys came marching up the aisle, Tom in the lead, Joe next, and Huck in the rear! They had been hid in the unused gallery listening to their own funeral sermon!

Aunt Polly, Mary, and the Harpers threw themselves

upon their restored ones, smothered them with kisses, and poured out thanksgiving. Poor Huck stood back, not knowing what to do or where to hide from so many eyes. He hesitated, then started to move away, but Tom seized him and said:

"Aunt Polly, it isn't fair! Somebody's got to be glad to see Huck!"

"And so they shall. *I'm* glad to see him, poor motherless thing!" And the loving attentions Aunt Polly gave Huck made him more uncomfortable than he was before.

Suddenly the minister shouted at the top of his voice:

"Praise God, from whom all blessings flow! SING! And put your hearts in it!"

And sing they did. The song nearly shook the rafters, and as the people left the church they said it would be a long time before the song would be sung like that once more.

Tom Sawyer, the Pirate, looked around upon the envying young people about him and confessed in his heart that this was the proudest moment of his life. He got more slaps and kisses that day—according to the way Aunt Polly felt—than he had earned before in a year. And he hardly knew which showed the most—gratefulness to God or love for himself.

18 Everybody Loves a Hero —Except Becky

That was Tom's great secret—the plan to return home with his brother pirates and attend their own funerals. They had paddled over to the shore on a log the night before, slept in the woods at the edge of town till nearly daylight, and then crept through back alleys to the church to finish their sleep in the gallery.

At breakfast on Monday morning Aunt Polly and Mary were very loving to Tom. There was much talk. In the course of it Aunt Polly said:

"Well, I don't say it wasn't a fine joke, Tom, but it is a pity you could be so hard-hearted as to let *me* suffer so. If you could come over on a log to go to your funeral, you could have come over and given me a hint some way that you weren't *dead,* but had only run off."

"Yes, you could have done that, Tom," said Mary. "I believe you would if you had thought of it."

"I—well, I don't know. It would have spoiled everything!"

"More's the pity," remarked Aunt Polly. "Sid would have thought. And Sid would have come and *done* it, too. Tom, you'll look back, some day, when it's too late, and wish you'd cared a little more for me when it would have cost you so little."

"Now, auntie, you know I do care for you!" declared Tom.

"I'd know it better if you acted more like it."

"I wish now I'd thought," said Tom. "But I dreamed about you, anyway. That's something, isn't it?"

"It isn't much—a cat does that much—but it's better than nothing. What did you dream?"

"Why, Wednesday night I dreamed that you were sitting there by the couch, and Sid was sitting here, and Mary next to him."

"Well, so we did. So we always do. I'm glad your dreams could take even that much trouble about us."

"And I dreamed that Joe Harper's mother was here."

"Why, she *was* here! Did you dream any more?"

"Oh, lots. But it's so dim, now. Somehow it seems to me that the wind blew the candle out."

"Mercy on us! Go on, Tom—go on!"

"And it seems to me you said, 'Why, I believe the door is open.'"

"As I'm sitting here, I did! Didn't I, Mary? Go on!"

"And then—and then—it seems like you made Sid go and shut the door."

"Well, for the land's sake! Don't tell *me* there isn't anything in dreams, anymore. Sereny Harper shall know of this before I'm an hour older. Go on, Tom!"

"Oh, it's all getting just as bright as day, now. Next you said I wasn't bad, only full of life, like a colt, or something. And then you began to cry."

"So I did! So I did. Not the first time, neither. And then—"

"Then Mrs. Harper began to cry, and said she wished she hadn't whipped Joe for taking cream when she'd thrown it out her own self—"

"Tom! The spirit was upon you! Land alive, go on, Tom!"

"Then Sid said—"

"I don't think I said anything," said Sid.

"Yes, you did, Sid!" said Mary.

"Shut up, both of you, and let Tom go on! What did he say, Tom?"

"He said—I *think* he said he hoped I was better off where I was gone to, but if I'd been better, sometimes—"

"*There*, do you hear that? His very words!"

"And you shut him up sharp."

"I'll say I did!"

"And Mrs. Harper told about Joe scaring her with a firecracker, and you told about Peter and the Painkiller—"

"Just as true as I live!"

"And then there was a whole lot of talk about dragging the river for us, and about having the funeral Sunday. And then you and old Mrs. Harper hugged and cried, and she went."

"It happened just so! Tom, you couldn't have told it better if you'd seen it! And *then* what, Tom?"

"Then I thought you prayed for me—and I could see you and hear every word you said. And you went to bed, and I was so sorry I took and wrote on a piece of bark, '*We aren't dead—we are only being pirates,*' and put it on the table. And you looked so good there, asleep, that I thought I went and leaned over and kissed you."

"Did you, Tom, *did* you! I just forgive you *everything* for that!" And she seized Tom and hugged him so hard she nearly crushed him. "Here's a big apple I've been saving for you, Tom, if you were ever found again. I'm thankful to the good God and Father of us all I've got you back. Go along, now, to school—all of you."

The children left for school, and the old lady went to call on Mrs. Harper to tell her all about Tom's marvelous dream. Sid said nothing, but he thought: "Such a long dream—and without any mistakes in it!"

What a hero Tom was, now! The smaller boys followed at his heels, proud to be seen with him. The older boys pretended not to know he had been away at all, but they would have given anything to have his sun-tanned skin or to have been with him.

At school the children made so much of him and of Joe that the two heroes were not long in becoming stuck-up. Their stories got bigger—and longer—and finally, when the two boys got out their pipes and took a puff, the top of their glory was reached.

Tom decided that he could get along without Becky Thatcher now. He would live for glory. Now that he was important, maybe she would want to make up. Well, let her—she would see that he could act as if he didn't care—like some other people.

Presently Becky arrived on the school grounds. Tom pretended not to see her and moved away to talk to some boys and girls. He noticed, though, as she was playing, that she was moving closer to him all the time. At last she stopped her playing and looked at Tom, but he managed to be talking more to Amy Lawrence than to anyone else at that time.

Becky felt a sharp pain. She tried to go away, but her feet carried her right to the group instead. She said to a girl almost at Tom's elbow:

"Why, Mary Austin! You bad girl, why didn't you come to Sunday School?"

"I did come—didn't you see me?"

"Why, no! Did you? Where did you sit?"

"I was in Miss Peters's class, where I always go. I saw *you*."

"Did you? Why, it's funny I didn't see you—I wanted to tell you about the picnic."

"Oh, that's nice. Who's going to give it?"

"My mother is going to let me have one."

"Oh, goody! I hope she'll let *me* come."

"Well, she will. The picnic is for me. She'll let anybody come that I want, and I want you."

"That's ever so nice. When is it going to be?"

"By and by. Maybe about vacation."

"Oh, won't that be fun! Are you going to have all the girls and boys?"

"Yes, every one that's friends to me—or wants to be." She glanced at Tom, but he kept right on talking to Amy Lawrence about the terrible storm on the island and how lightning tore a tree "all to flinders" while he was three feet from it.

All of the group begged to come to the picnic—but Tom and Amy. Tom turned coolly away, still talking, and took Amy with him. Becky's lips trembled and tears came to her eyes, but she hid the way she felt and kept on talking. She didn't care about the picnic, now. She got away as soon as she could and hid herself and had a good cry. Then she gave her head a shake and said she knew what *she'd* do.

At recess, Tom went around with Amy again. He kept drifting about to find Becky so that she could see. At last he found her, but what he saw he didn't like, for Becky was sitting on a little bench behind the schoolhouse looking at a comic book with another boy, Alfred Temple—and their heads were close together!

Tom began to hate himself for not making up with Becky. He walked around to the back of the schoolhouse again and again with Amy, but Becky looked as if she didn't know Tom was even alive. But she did see him.

Tom, at last, couldn't stand Amy's empty talk anymore. He got away from her by telling her he had other things to do. She said she would be around when school let out, but he hurried away, hating her for it. Alone,

Tom made believe he was fighting with another boy, even going through the motions, until the fight was finished to his satisfaction.

Tom fled home at noon. He couldn't stand any more of Amy or of Becky's new boyfriend. Becky went on looking at the picture book with Alfred, but when she didn't see Tom, she lost interest. At last she didn't care about the book at all, and when Alfred said, "Oh, here's a good picture—look at this!" she told him, "Oh, don't bother me! I don't care for them!" She burst into tears, got up, and walked away.

Alfred tried to comfort her, but she said:

"Go away and leave me alone, can't you! I hate you!"

Alfred stopped, wondering what he could have done. He easily guessed at the truth—that Becky had been with him because she was angry with Tom Sawyer. Alfred wished there was some way he could get back at Tom. He saw Tom's spelling book, took it, opened it to the lesson for the afternoon, and poured ink upon the page.

Becky, looking in at a window behind Alfred at the same time, saw the act. She started homeward, now, with plans to find Tom and tell him. Before she was half-way home, however, she changed her mind when she thought of the way Tom had treated her when she was talking about her picnic. She decided to let him get whipped for the spelling book, and to hate him forever, too.

19 *Aunt Polly Ends Her Doubts*

Tom arrived at home feeling gloomy, and the first thing his Aunt Polly said to him didn't make him feel any better:

"Tom, I've a notion to skin you alive!"

"Why, auntie, what have I done?"

"Well, you've done enough. Here I go over to Sereny Harper, like an old softy, expecting I'm going to make her believe all that stuff about that dream, when lo and behold she'd found out from Joe that you were over here and heard all the talk we had that night! Tom, I don't know what's to become of a boy that will act like that. It makes me feel so bad to think you could let me go and make such a fool of myself and never say a word!"

This was something new for Tom to think about. The dream had seemed a good joke to Tom before, and very clever, but now it looked mean and unfair. He hung his head and could not think of anything to say for a moment. Then he said:

"Auntie, I wish I hadn't done it—but, I didn't think."

"Oh, child, you never think! You never think of anything but yourself. But you could think to come all the way over here from Jackson's Island in the night to laugh at our troubles, and you could think to fool me with a lie about a dream. But you couldn't ever think to pity us and save us from sorrow!"

"Auntie, I know now it was mean, but I didn't mean to be. I didn't, honest. And besides, I didn't come over here to laugh at you that night."

"What did you come for, then?"

"It was to tell you not to be uneasy about us, because we hadn't drowned."

"Tom, I'd thank the world if I could believe you ever had as good a thought as that, but you know you never did—and I know it, Tom."

"But it's the truth! I wanted to keep you from grieving—that was all that made me come."

"I'd give the whole world to believe that, Tom. I'd almost be glad that you'd run off and acted so bad. But it doesn't seem possible, because, why didn't you tell me, child?"

"Why, you see, when you got to talking about the funeral, I just got all full of the idea of our coming and hiding in the church, and I couldn't bear to spoil it. So, I just put the bark note back in my jacket pocket and kept mum."

"What bark?"

"The bark I wrote on to tell you we'd gone pirating. I wish, now, you'd have waked up when I kissed you—I do, honest."

Aunt Polly didn't look quite so angry, now. A soft look came into her eyes.

"*Did* you kiss me, Tom?"

"Why, yes, I did."

"Are you sure you did, Tom?"

"Why, yes I did, auntie—certain sure!"

"What did you kiss me for, Tom?"

"Because I loved you so. And you lay there moaning and I was so sorry."

The words sounded like the truth. The old lady could not hide a shake in her voice when she said:

"Kiss me again, Tom!—and be off with you to school, now, and don't bother me any more."

The moment he was gone, she ran to the clothes closet and got out the old jacket Tom had used to go pirating in. She stopped a moment to think whether it was right to see if Tom had lied, but she made up her mind that even if he did, it was a good lie. Her hand went into the jacket pocket.

A moment later she was reading Tom's piece of bark through flowing tears and saying to herself: "I could forgive the boy, now, if he'd committed a million sins!"

20 Tom Becomes Becky's Noble Hero

There was something about Aunt Polly's way, when she kissed Tom, that swept away his troubles and made him light-hearted and happy again. He started to school and had the luck of meeting Becky Thatcher at the end of the street. The way he felt always decided what he would do, so he ran to her and said:

"I acted mighty mean today, Becky, and I'm so sorry. I won't ever, ever do that again, as long as I live! Please make up, won't you?"

The girl stopped and looked him coldly in the face. "I'll thank you to keep yourself *to* yourself, Mr. Thomas Sawyer. I'll never speak to you again!" she declared, tossed her head, and moved on.

Tom was so stunned that he didn't even think fast enough to say, "Who cares, Miss Smarty?" In fact, he said nothing. But he was in a rage and wished that she were a boy—how he would beat her up! He presently met her in the schoolyard and called her names as she passed. She threw one back. The break was complete. Becky could hardly wait for school to begin again so that Tom would get whipped for the ink on his spelling book.

Poor girl, she didn't know how fast she was going to get into trouble herself! The schoolteacher, Mr. Dobbins, had always wanted to be a doctor. Every day he took a mysterious book out of his desk when he had spare time and read it. He kept that book under lock and key. There wasn't child in school but who was dying to get a look at it, but the chance never came.

But now, as Becky was passing the desk, she saw that the key was in the lock—and the teacher wasn't around! The next instant she had the secret book in her hands. She didn't know what the title, Professor Somebody's *Anatomy,* meant, so she began to turn the leaves. The first thing she saw was a colored picture of a human figure without any clothes on.

At that moment, a shadow fell on the page, and Tom Sawyer stepped in at the door and saw the picture too. Becky grabbed at the book to close it, and the picture tore half way down the middle! She pushed the book into the desk, turned the key, and burst out crying:

"Tom Sawyer, you are just as mean as you can be, to sneak up on a person and look at what she's looking at!"

"How could *I* know you were looking at anything?"

"You ought to be ashamed of yourself, Tom Sawyer! You know you're going to tell on me, and I'll be whipped, and I was never whipped in my life!"

Then she stamped her little foot and said:

"*Be* so mean, if you want to! *I* know something that's going to happen to you—you just wait and you'll see! Hateful, hateful, hateful!" She flung herself out of the schoolhouse with a new burst of crying.

Tom stood still, a little mixed up. Then he said to himself: "Girls are funny! Never been licked in school? Shucks. What's a licking! But I won't tell on her, because there are other ways of getting even. Old Dobbins will find out. He'll ask first one, and then the other, and when he comes to the right girl, he'll know it, without any telling. Girls' faces always tell on them. She'll get licked! All right, though—she'd like to see me in just such a fix— let her sweat it out!"

Tom joined the other students who were playing outside. In a few moments the teacher arrived and school began. Tom didn't feel like studying—he watched Becky. He did not want to pity her but he couldn't help it.

Presently the ink on his spelling book was noticed, and Tom was busy with his own troubles for a while after that. Becky didn't expect Tom to get out of his trouble by saying he didn't spill the ink himself, and she was right. She wanted to tell on Alfred Temple when Tom got his whipping, but she said to herself: "Tom will tell on me for tearing the picture, for sure. I won't say a word, not to save his life!"

When Tom went back to his seat after his whipping, he wasn't broken-hearted at all, for he thought that he might have spilled the ink himself without knowing it. Of course he said he didn't—but he always did that no matter what!

An hour went by. The teacher, at last, found a little time, unlocked his desk, and reached for his book. He settled himself in his chair, ready to open the book and read it.

Tom shot a glance at Becky. He saw that she looked scared, like a rabbit does when it is hunted. He forgot his quarrel with her. He must do something.

The next moment the teacher faced the school. There was anger in his eye. The room became silent. He demanded:

"Who tore this book?"

There was not a sound. One could have heard a pin drop. The teacher looked from face to face to find the guilty one. He asked:

"Benjamin Rogers, did you tear this book?"

Ben said no. The teacher waited, then asked:

"Joseph Harper, did you?"

"No, sir!"

Tom grew more and more disturbed as the teacher

looked over the boys—thought a while—and then turned to the girls. He went on:

"Amy Lawrence?"

Amy shook her head.

"Gracie Miller?"

She made the same sign.

"Susan Harper, did you do this?"

"No, sir!"

The next girl was Becky Thatcher. Tom was trembling from head to foot with excitement. What could he do?

"Rebecca Thatcher—"

Tom looked at Becky's face—it was white with terror.

"—Did you tear—"

Becky lowered her eyes.

"—No, look me in the face—"

Her hands rose in appeal.

"—Did you tear this book?"

A thought shot like lightning through Tom's mind. He sprang to his feet and shouted:

"I did it!"

The school stared in wonder. Tom stood a moment to get hold of himself, then stepped forward to go to his punishment. The look that came from poor Becky's eyes was enough to pay him for a hundred whippings. He took the punishment without a cry and didn't even mind the command to stay two hours after school. He knew Becky would wait for him outside.

That night Tom went to bed planning to get even with Alfred for putting the ink on Tom's speller, for Becky had told him all about it. He fell asleep, at last, with Becky's latest words playing like music in his ears—"Tom, how *could* you be so noble!"

21   School Breaks Up
—For Vacation

Vacation was approaching. The schoolteacher, always severe, made everybody work harder, for he wanted the school to make a good showing when the parents came to visit on the last day. His switch and ruler were used on everybody except the biggest boys and the oldest girls. And Mr. Dobbins hit hard, too, for although he was bald—he wore a wig to cover his shiny head—he had plenty of muscle.

As the big day came near, he grew worse, and punished everyone for the least little thing. The smaller boys spent their days in fear and their nights planning to get even. They tried every trick they knew to make trouble for the teacher, but he kept ahead of them all the time.

At last the boys got together and hit upon a plan that promised to work. They asked the sign painter's son to help. He said he would. Since the teacher boarded at the sign painter's house, the boy said he would work the plan while the teacher took a nap before the time he left for school.

In time the interesting occasion arrived. At eight in the evening the schoolhouse was brightly lighted, and leaves and flowers were everywhere. The teacher sat like a king in his great chair on the raised platform, the blackboard behind him. The schoolchildren, all dressed up, were in special seats up front. All the rest of the room was filled with parents and friends.

The program began. A very little boy stood up and

began, "You'd scarce expect one of my age to speak in public on the stage." He was scared but he got through his speech all right, although he made funny motions. The people clapped their hands for him when he finished and made a bow.

A shy little girl came next to give "Mary had a little lamb." As she finished, she made a big bow, too.

Tom Sawyer stepped forward and started "Give me liberty or give me death" with confidence and much waving of his arms. He broke down in the middle of it and couldn't remember the rest of the words. He struggled awhile, but at last sat down, defeated.

"The Boy Stood on the Burning Deck" followed. Other poems also were given. Then there were reading exercises, and a spelldown. The Latin class said some words. At last the older girls read the papers they had written themselves. A prize was to be given for the best one.

The papers were about many things. Some were sad. One was a poem. Some had long words in them even the girls using them didn't know. Others had fine words. All had lessons from life at the end. The paper that won was ten pages long.

Now the teacher turned to the blackboard to draw a map of America on it so he could test the geography class. His first drawing wasn't quite right, and the people laughed a little. He erased part of the map and drew it over. The people still laughed. He couldn't understand it. He tried drawing the map the third time. The laughing was louder.

And well it might, for above him, from an opening in the ceiling, came a cat, held by a string! The cat, as it came closer and closer to the teacher's head, clawed at the string and the air, but it made no sound for a cloth had been tied about its head and jaws.

The laughing grew louder and louder. The cat came down within six inches of the teacher's head, but he was still busy drawing the map. At last the cat was nearly on his head. Down, down, a little lower—the cat grabbed his wig with its claws, clung to it, and was snatched up through the hole in the ceiling in an instant!

How the light did shine from the teacher's bald head—the sign painter's boy had painted it with gold paint! The boys had gotten even.

That broke up the meeting. Vacation had come.

22 The Boys Change —And Change Again

Tom joined a new club, The Cadets, for the summer. He liked the showy uniform the club members wore. He promised not to smoke, chew, or swear as long as he remained a member.

Now he found out a new thing. Since he had promised not to swear or smoke, he wanted to more than ever. But he wanted to march in his new uniform, and that kept him from quitting the club.

The Fourth of July was coming, but Tom wanted to march before then. There was a chance that old Judge Frazer would die soon and have a big public funeral. The Cadets always marched at important affairs like that. Tom hoped every day he would hear news about the death of the Judge, and got out his uniform to practice marching before the looking glass.

But the Judge fooled everyone. He got better. Tom was disgusted. He quit the club. That same night the Judge got sick again and died. Tom made up his mind he would never trust a man like that again.

The funeral was a fine thing. The Cadets marched in fine style. But not Tom—he was a free boy again. There was something in that. But Tom found, to his surprise, that now that he could swear, smoke, and drink, he didn't want to.

Tom presently wondered what to do during his vacation. Time was passing too slowly for him. He tried keeping a diary and writing down what he did from day to day—but nothing happened for three days, so he gave that up.

A traveling show came to town. Then there was excitement. Tom and Joe Harper got up a show of their own and were happy for two days.

Even the Glorious Fourth fell short of what Tom expected. It rained hard. As a result, there was no parade, nor fireworks. Even the important speaker for the day, a real United States Senator, wasn't twenty-five feet high, as Tom supposed, but just an ordinary man.

A circus came. Afterwards the boys played circus for three days in tents made of carpets. They charged admission. Boys had to pay three pins, the girls two.

A fortuneteller, and a man who could put people to sleep, came. They went again. The village was duller than ever.

There were some parties to which both boys and girls were invited. But, they were so few and so much fun that waiting for the next one only made the time between pass so much slower.

Becky Thatcher had gone away to another town for her vacation. There was no bright side to life for Tom anywhere.

The dreadful secret of the murder in the graveyard still troubled Tom. It was always on his mind.

Then came the measles.

Tom was sick in bed for two weeks. He was very sick, and didn't care what happened. When he got upon his feet, at last, and took a walk downtown, everything seemed changed.

There had been a special church service and everybody had gotten religion, even the boys and girls. Tom found Joe Harper studying a part of the Bible. Tom looked for Ben Rogers, and found him taking little religious books around. Jim Hollis told Tom his late sickness was a warning.

At last Tom flew to Huckleberry Finn. Huck's first words were from the Bible. That did it. Tom crept home and to bed realizing that he, of all the town, was lost, forever and forever.

And that night there came a terrible storm, with much rain, awful thunder, and blinding lightning. Tom covered his head with the bedclothes and waited in terror for his end. He felt sure the storm had been sent for him.

By and by the storm died out. Tom found himself still alive. His first thought was to be thankful, and be a better boy. His second thought was to wait—for there might not be any more storms!

The next day the doctors were back. Tom had gotten sick again. This time he spent three weeks on his back. The time seemed an age. When he was able to go out, at last, he wasn't sure that he should be grateful for being alive. He remembered how lonely he had been, as a bad boy, and how good all his friends were, now.

He wandered down the street, not interested in anything. He found Jim Hollis acting as a judge that was trying a cat for murdering a bird. A little later he found Joe Harper and Huck Finn up an alley eating a stolen melon. Tom wasn't lonely any more.

23 Potter's Trial Ends With a Crash

At last the sleepy air was stirred strongly—the murder trial came up in court. Everybody talked about it. Tom couldn't get away from it. He felt sure people talked about the murder so that he would tell what he knew about it. It kept him in a cold shiver all the time.

He took Huck to a lonely place to have a talk with him. He wanted to be sure that Huck hadn't told their secret.

"Huck, have you ever told anybody about—that?"

"Oh—'course I haven't."

"Never a word?"

"Never a single word! Why?"

"Well, I was afraid."

"Why, Tom Sawyer, we wouldn't be alive two days if that got out! *You* know that."

Tom felt more comfortable. After a pause, he said:

"Huck, they couldn't get you to tell, could they?"

"Get me to tell? Why, if Injun Joe drowned me they could get me to tell, but no other way."

"Well, that's all right, then, I guess we're safe as long as we keep mum. But let's swear again, to make sure."

"I'm agreed."

They swore again with serious feelings.

"What's the talk, Huck? I've heard a lot of it."

"Talk? Well, it's just Muff Potter, Muff Potter, Muff Potter, all the time. It keeps me scared so I want to hide somewheres!"

"That's the same as I hear. I guess he's a goner. Don't you feel sorry for him, sometimes?"

" 'Most always. He's no account, but then, he hasn't ever done anything to hurt anybody. He doesn't work much, but he's kind and good. He gave me half a fish, once, when there wasn't enough for two. Lots of times he's stood by me when I was out of luck."

"Well, he's fixed kites for me, Huck, and put hooks on my line. I wish we could get him out of there!"

"My! we couldn't get him out, Tom. Besides, it wouldn't do any good. They'd catch him again."

"Yes, so they would. But I hate to hear people talk about him when we know he never did it."

The boys had a long talk, but it brought them little comfort. At the end of the day they found themselves at the little jail, hoping that something would happen to clear the way for Potter. But nothing happened. No one was interested in poor old Muff.

The boys went to the cell window and gave Potter some tobacco and matches through the open bars. He was on the ground floor and there were no guards. He was very thankful, and said:

"You've been mighty good to me, boys, better than anybody else in this town. And I won't forget it, I won't. They've all forgot old Muff when he's in trouble. But Tom and Huck don't. *They* don't forget me. Well, boys, I did an awful thing. Now I got to swing for it. And it's right—right, and *best*, too. I guess. Well, we won't talk about that. I don't want to make *you* feel bad. You are my friends. Shake hands."

Tom went home unhappy. His dreams that night were full of horrors. The next day, and the day after that, he hung around the courthouse wanting to go in but staying out. Huck was having the same trouble. They kept away from each other, and from time to time even left the courthouse, but always came back.

Tom kept his ears open when people left the courtroom so he could get news of what was happening. The evidence was closing more and more around poor Potter. What Injun Joe had said against him still stood. At the end of the second day the village was sure Muff Potter would be judged guilty.

That night, Tom was out late. He came to bed through the window. He was very excited, and it was hours before he got to sleep.

The next morning all the village was at the courthouse, for this was to be the great day. The courtroom was packed. Muff Potter was brought in, pale, thin, and without hope. There were chains on his legs and arms. Injun Joe was there, too.

The trial continued. Witnesses were called and said that Muff Potter had washed in the brook at an early hour the morning that the murder was discovered, and that the knife found near the body was his. Others told of his actions in the graveyard the morning of the murder. At last the lawyer trying to prove Potter guilty said:

"We have fastened this awful crime on the prisoner. We rest our case here."

A groan came from poor Potter. He put his face in his hands. The courtroom was silent. Potter's lawyer rose and said:

"Call Thomas Sawyer!"

There was surprise on every face, even Potter's. Every eye was on Tom as he rose and took his place upon the witness stand. The boy looked wild, for he was badly scared. Potter's lawyer asked:

"Thomas Sawyer, where were you on the seventeenth of June, about the hour of midnight?"

Tom glanced at Injun Joe's iron face and his tongue failed him. The people listened, but the words wouldn't come. After a few moments, however, Tom got a little of his strength back and whispered:

"In the graveyard!"

"A little bit louder, please. Don't be afraid. You were—"

"In the graveyard."

Injun Joe smiled.

"Were you anywhere near Horse William's grave?"

"Yes, sir."

"Speak up—just a trifle louder. How near were you?"

"Near as I am to you."

"Were you hidden, or not?"

"I was hid."

"Where?"

"Behind the elms that's on the edge of the grave."

Injun Joe moved a little.

"Anyone with you?"

"Yes, sir. I went there with—"

"Wait—wait a minute! Never mind mentioning your companion's name. We will produce him at the proper time. Did you carry anything there with you?"

Tom hesitated and looked ashamed.

"Speak out, my boy—don't be shy. The truth is always good. What did you take there?"

"Only a—a—dead cat."

"We will produce the bones of that cat. Now, my boy, tell us everything that occurred. Tell it in your own way. Don't skip anything, and don't be afraid."

Tom began, slowly at first, but soon his words came easily. Every ear, every eye was fixed upon him as the people listened to his story. At last he came to the murder and said:

"—And as the doctor grabbed the board and hit Muff Potter on the head, Muff fell, and Injun Joe jumped with the knife and—"

Crash! Quick as lightning Injun Joe sprang for a window, got away from people who tried to stop him, and was gone!

24 *Injun Joe*
Haunts Tom's Dreams

Tom was a glittering hero once more, both with the old and the young. His name even went into print, for the village paper wrote about him. There were some that believed that he might be President, yet, some day.

Muff Potter was forgiven. People were as good to him now, and remembered him, as they had been bad to him and forgotten him before.

Tom's days were days of glory and joy to him, but his nights were times of terror. Injun Joe was in all his dreams, and always Injun Joe had murder in his eye. Nothing could get Tom to go out after dark.

Poor Huck was the same way, for Tom had told the whole story to the lawyer the night before the great day of the trial, and Huck was afraid that his share in the business might leak out. Even though Injun Joe had escaped from the trial and Huck didn't have to tell anything, Huck was still afraid. Besides, since Tom had told the story he had promised Huck he wouldn't tell, Huck's confidence in the human race was wiped out.

Daily Muff Potter's thanks made Tom glad he had spoken. But, nightly, when the dreams came, Tom wished he had sealed up his tongue.

Half the time Tom wished Injun Joe would never be captured. The other half he was afraid Injun Joe would be. Tom felt sure he never could draw a safe breath again until that man was dead and Tom could see the body.

Rewards had been offered, the country had been searched, but no Injun Joe was found, not even a trace. Tom did not feel safe.

The slow days drifted on, and each left behind it a little less fear than the day before.

25 The Search for Buried Treasure Begins

The desire to go somewhere and dig for hidden treasure suddenly came upon Tom one day. He rushed out to find Joe Harper, but failed of success. Next he looked for Ben Rogers. Ben had gone fishing. Presently he ran across Huck Finn. Huck was willing. Huck was always willing to do anything—if it didn't cost anything—he had a lot of time, but no money.

"Where'll we dig?" asked Huck.

"Oh, most anywhere."

"Why, is it hid all around?"

"No, indeed it isn't. It's hid in mighty particular places, Huck—sometimes on islands, sometimes in rotten chests under the end of a limb of an old dead tree, just where the shadow falls at midnight. But mostly it's hid under the floor in haunted houses."

"Who hides it?"

"Why, robbers, of course! Who'd you think?"

"I don't know. If it was mine, I wouldn't hide it— I'd spend it and have a good time!"

"So would I. But robbers don't do it that way. They always hide it and leave it there."

"Don't they come after it?"

"No, they think they will, but they generally forget the place, or else they die. Anyway, it's there a long time, and gets rusty. But by and by somebody finds an old yellow paper that tells how to find it by the marks on it."

"Have you found any old papers, Tom?"

"No."

"Well, then, how are you going to find the treasure?"

"Why, they always bury it under a haunted house, or on an island, or under a dead tree that's got one limb sticking out. We've tried the island. Let's try the big hill, first. There's lots of dead-limb trees there, loads of 'em!"

"Is it under all of them?"

"How you talk! No!"

"Then how are you going to know which one to go for?"

"Go for all of 'em!"

"Why, Tom, that'll take all summer!"

"Well, what of that? Suppose you find a pot with a hundred dollars in it, all rusty, or a rotten chest full of diamonds. How's that?"

Huck's eyes glowed.

"That's bully! But you just give me the hundred dollars. I don't want the diamonds."

"All right. But I'm not going to throw away the diamonds! Some of 'em are worth twenty dollars apiece."

"No! Is that so?"

"Certainly. Anybody will tell you so. Kings have lots of 'em."

"Well, maybe. But say—where you going to dig first?"

"Well, I don't know. Suppose we tackle that biggest old dead-limb tree on the hill the other side of the slope."

"I'm agreed."

So they got an old pick and a shovel, and set out on the three-mile hike to the big hill. They arrived hot and panting and threw themselves down in the shade of a neighboring elm to rest.

"I like this," said Tom.

"So do I."

"Say, Huck, if we find a treasure here, what are you going to do with your share?"

"Well, I'll have pie and soda every day, and I'll go to every circus that comes along!"

"Aren't you going to save any of it?"

"Save it? What for?"

"Why, to have something to live on, by and by!"

"Oh, that's no use. My pop would come back to town some day and clean it out pretty quick. What are you going to do with yours, Tom?"

"I'm going to buy a drum, a sword, a red necktie, a bull pup, and get married."

"Married?"

"That's it."

"Tom, you—why, you aren't in your right mind!"

"Wait—you'll see!"

"Well, that's the foolishest thing you could do! And if you get married, I'll be more lonesomer than ever."

"No, you won't—you'll come and live with me. Now stir out of this, and we'll start digging."

They worked and worked for half an hour. No result. They toiled another half hour. Still no result. Huck said:

"Do they always bury it as deep as this?"

"Sometimes—not always. I guess we haven't got the right place."

The boys chose a new spot, and began again. The labor dragged a little, but still they dug. Finally Huck leaned on his shovel, wiped the drops from his brow with his sleeve, and asked:

"Where you going to dig next, after we get this one?"

"I guess maybe we'll tackle the old tree that's on the hill in back of the widow's house."

"I guess that'll be a good one. But won't the widow take it away from us, Tom? It's on her land."

"*She* take it away! Whoever finds one of these hid treasures, it belongs to him. It doesn't make any difference whose land it's on."

Huck was satisfied. The work went on. By and by Huck said:

"Blame it, we must be in the wrong place again, Tom! What do you think?"

"It *is* mighty curious, Huck. Oh, *I* know what the matter is! You got to find out where the shadow of the limb falls at midnight, and that's where you dig!"

"Then we fooled away all this work for nothing? Now, hang it all, we got to come back in the night. It's an awful long way, too. Can you get out?"

"I bet I will. We've got to do it tonight, too, because if somebody sees these holes they'll know in a minute what's here and they'll go for it!"

"Well, I'll come around and meow tonight."

"All right. Let's hide the tools in the bushes."

That night the boys were there again, near midnight. They sat in the dark, waiting for the moon to make a shadow of the limb. At last the shadow fell and they began to dig. They worked hard and the hole deepened and deepened. Their hearts jumped every time the pick struck something, but they found only stone or chunks of rock. At last Tom said:

"It's no use, Huck. We're wrong again."

"Well, but we *can't* be wrong! We spotted the shadow to a dot."

"I know it, but there's another thing—we only guessed at the time. Like enough it was too late or too early."

Huck dropped his shovel.

"That's it!" said he. "That's the very trouble. We got to give this one up. Where'll we go?"

Tom considered a while, and then said:

"The haunted house. That's it!"

"Blame it, I don't like haunted houses, Tom! Why, haunted houses are worse than dead people because ghosts come sliding around when you aren't noticing and peek over your shoulder all of a sudden and grit their teeth. I couldn't stand such a thing as that, Tom —nobody could!"

"Yes, but Huck, ghosts travel around only at night. They won't keep us from digging there in the daytime."

"Well, that's so. But you know mighty well people don't go around that haunted house in the day nor the night!"

"That's mostly because they don't like to go where a man's been murdered. But nothing's ever been seen around that house except in the night—just some blue lights slipping by the windows—no regular ghosts."

"Well, where you see one of those blue lights around, Tom, you can bet there's a ghost mighty close behind it! It stands to reason. *You* know that nobody but ghosts uses 'em."

"Yes, that's so. But anyway, they don't come around in the daytime, so what's the use of being afraid?"

"Well, all right. We'll tackle the haunted house if you say so—but I guess it's taking chances."

They had started down the hill by this time. There, in the moonlit valley below them, stood the haunted house, alone, its fence fallen down, weeds around it, the chimney broken, the windows smashed, a corner of the roof caved in. The boys looked awhile, expecting to see a blue light in the window. Then, talking in a low tone, they took their way homeward by taking the long way—to keep as far away from the haunted house as they could.

26 Treasure—And Trouble —Are Found

About noon, the next day, the boys were back at the dead tree. They had come for their tools. Both wanted to get to the haunted house as fast as they could, but suddenly Huck said:

"Look, Tom, do you know what day this is?"

Tom thought, then quickly lifted his eyes with a surprised look in them and exclaimed:

"My! I never once thought of it, Huck! We can't tackle this thing on a Friday!"

"And Friday isn't all, either. I had a rotten bad dream last night—I dreamed of rats!"

"No! Sure sign of trouble. Did they fight?"

"No."

"Well, that's good, Huck. When they don't fight it's only a sign that there's trouble around. All we got to do is to look mighty sharp and keep out of it. We'll drop this thing for today, and play."

They played Robin Hood all the afternoon. But now and then they cast a wishful eye upon the haunted house and talked about the heaps of treasure buried there. As the sun began to sink into the west, they took their way homeward.

The next day, Saturday, shortly after noon, the boys were at the dead tree again. They dug a little more in their last hole before they started for the haunted house because Tom said there were many cases where people stopped digging after getting down to within six inches of the treasure. Then, somebody else had come along and turned it up with a single dig of the shovel. But, the thing failed this time.

When they reached the haunted house there was something about it that made them afraid to go in. At last they crept to the door and took a trembling peep. They saw nothing but an empty room and here, there, and everywhere ragged spider webs.

They presently entered, softly, with hearts pounding, talking in whispers, ears open to catch the slightest sound, and ready to turn and run. But in a little while they became bold, and looked around carefully.

Next they wanted to look upstairs. They dared each other, and, of course, there could be but one result—they threw their tools into a corner and went up.

Upstairs they found nothing new except a closed closet door. They opened it—there was nothing in the closet. Their courage was up now and well in hand. They were about to go down and begin work when—

"S-s-h!" said Tom.

"What is it?" whispered Huck, turning white with fright.

"Sh! . . . There! . . . Hear it?"

"Yes! . . . Oh, my! Let's run!"

"Keep still! Don't budge! They're coming right toward the door!"

The boys stretched themselves upon the floor with their eyes to the cracks in the boards in order to see downstairs. They lay waiting, in fear.

"They've stopped—no, coming! . . . Don't whisper another word, Huck! My goodness, I wish I were out of this!"

Two men entered the haunted house. Each boy said to himself, "There's the old deaf and dumb Spaniard that's been around town once or twice lately—never saw the other man before."

The other was a ragged, dirty man, with nothing very pleasant in his face. The Spaniard was wrapped in a blanket. He had long white whiskers and hair. A big hat covered his head, and he wore green goggles.

When they came in, the other man was talking in a low voice. They sat down inside, facing the door, with their backs to the wall. The other man went on talking, a little louder.

"No," said he, "I've thought it all over, and I don't like it. It's dangerous."

"Dangerous!" grunted the deaf and dumb Spaniard —to the vast surprise of the boys who thought he couldn't talk or hear. "Milksop!"

This voice made the boys catch their breath—it was Injun Joe's! There was silence for some time, then Joe said:

"What's any more dangerous than that job up yonder—but nothing's come of it."

"That's different. That was away up the river, and not another house was around."

"Well, what's more dangerous than coming here in the daytime! Anybody would suspect us, that saw us."

"I know that, but there wasn't any other place as handy after that last job. I want to get out of here, and would have, yesterday, if those fool boys hadn't been playing over there on the hill where they could see us."

The boys shook when they heard this, and thought how lucky it was that they had remembered it was Friday and concluded to wait a day. Now they wished they had waited a year!

The two men got out some food and made a lunch. After a long silence, Injun Joe said:

"Look here, lad—you go back up the river where you belong. Wait there till you hear from me. I'll take the chance and drop into town just once more, for a look. We'll do that job after I've spied around. Then we'll head for Texas, together!"

This was satisfactory. Both men presently fell to yawning, and Injun Joe said:

"I'm dead for sleep! It's your turn to watch."

He curled down on the floor and soon began to snore. His comrade stirred him once or twice and Injun Joe became quiet. But at last the watcher began to nod. His head drooped lower and lower. Both men began to snore now.

The boys drew a long, thankful breath. Tom whispered:

"Now's our chance—come on!"

Huck said:

"I can't! I'd die if they woke up!"

Tom rose slowly and softly, and started alone. But the first step he made caused the floor to crack so loudly that he sank down almost dead with fright. He didn't try again.

The boys lay there, counting the minutes as they dragged by. It seemed that time must be done, it passed so slowly. At last they were grateful to note that the sun was setting.

Now one snore ceased. Injun Joe sat up, stared around, smiled grimly at his sleeping comrade, kicked him, and said:

"Here! *You* a watchman! All right, though—nothing's happened."

"Have I been asleep?"

"Partly—but it's time for us to be moving. What'll we do with the money we've got left?"

"I don't know—leave it here as we've always done, I guess. No use taking it away till we start south. Six hundred and fifty in silver is heavy to carry."

"Well—all right—it won't matter to come here once more."

"No—but I'd say come in the night as we used to do. It's better."

"Yes. But, look here—it may be a good while before I get the right chance at that job—accidents might happen. The money's not in such a very good place—we'll bury it, deep."

"Good idea!" said the comrade. He walked across the room, knelt down, raised one of the stones in front of the old fireplace, and took out a bag that jingled. He took from the bag some of the dollars for himself and as much for Injun Joe, then gave the bag to Joe.

Injun Joe was on his knees in the corner of the room digging a hole for the money with his big knife. Upstairs, the boys forgot all their fears, watching. Six hundred dollars was money enough to make half a dozen boys rich!

Joe's knife struck upon something.

"Hello!" said he.

"What is it?" asked his comrade.

"Half rotten plank—no, it's a box, I believe. Here—bear a hand and we'll see. Never mind—I broke a hole."

He reached his hand in and drew it out—

"Man, it's money!"

The two men looked and saw coins. They were gold. Huck and Tom above were as excited as the men below. Joe's comrade said:

"We'll make quick work of this—there's an old pick over in the other corner—I saw it a minute ago."

He ran and brought the boy's pick and shovel. Injun Joe took the pick, looked it over, shook his head, muttered something to himself, and then began to use it. The box was soon out. It wasn't very large, but it was

bound with iron and had been very strong once. The men looked at the treasure awhile in happy silence.

"Partner, there's thousands of dollars here!" said Injun Joe.

"It was always said a gang used to be around here one summer," replied the other.

"I know it," said Injun Joe, "and this looks like it, I should say."

"*Now* you won't need to do that job."

Injun Joe frowned, and said:

"You don't know me! At least, you don't know about one thing—it isn't robbery altogether—it's *revenge!*" A wicked light flamed in his eyes. "I'll need your help in it. When it's finished—then Texas! Go home and stand by till you hear from me."

"Well—if you say so. What'll we do with this—bury it again?"

"Yes."

The boys, overhead, were delighted.

"*No!* by the great chief, no!" Injun Joe added.

There was great sorrow overhead.

"I'd nearly forgot," Injun Joe went on. "That pick had fresh dirt on it!"

The boys were sick with terror in a moment.

"What business has a pick and a shovel here?" Joe asked. "Who brought them? No, we won't bury it again and leave them to come and dig it up! We'll take it to my den."

"Why, of course! Might have thought of that before. You mean Number One?"

"No—Number Two—under the cross. The other place is bad—too common."

"All right. It's nearly dark enough to start."

Injun Joe got up and went from window to window carefully looking out. Presently he said:

"Who could have brought those tools here? Do you think they can be upstairs?"

The boys stopped breathing. Injun Joe put his hand on his knife, stopped a moment, undecided, and then turned toward the stairway. The boys thought of the closet, but they couldn't move. They heard steps on the stairs.

Suddenly there was a crash of rotten wood. Injun Joe landed on the first floor as the stairway fell in. He got up, cursing. His comrade said:

"Now what's the use of all that? If anybody wants to jump down here and get into trouble, who cares? Whoever left those things in here and caught sight of us is probably running yet. It will be dark in fifteen minutes. Let them try to follow us, if they can!"

Joe muttered for a time, then agreed to use what

daylight was left to get ready to leave. Shortly after-
ward they slipped out of the house in the coming darkness, and moved toward the river with the precious
box.

Tom and Huck rose up, weak, but relieved. They
watched the men through holes between the logs of the
house until the men disappeared. Follow? Not they.
They were content to get outside again—and take the
other way, over the hill.

On the way home they didn't talk much. They were
too busy thinking and hating themselves for having
left the pick and the spade there for Injun Joe to see.
But for that, Injun Joe would never have suspected,
and the money would have been all theirs! They made
up their minds to keep a lookout for that Spaniard when
he came to do his revenge, and to follow him to "Number Two," wherever that might be.

Then a horrible thought occurred to Tom:

"Revenge? What if he means *us*, Huck!"

"Oh, don't!" said Huck, nearly fainting.

They talked it all over, and as they entered town
they agreed Injun Joe might have meant somebody else.
At least, he might mean no one but Tom, since Tom
had been the only one to talk at the trial. But it didn't
make Tom feel any better to think he alone was in
danger!

27 The Treasure Trail Is Found Again

The adventures of the day were in Tom's dreams that night. Four times he dreamed he had his hands on that rich treasure, and four times he awoke to find nothing in his fingers. As he lay in the early morning thinking of what had happened, it didn't seem real that there was so much money.

But as he thought things over, he knew what had happened had not been a dream, after all. He snatched a hurried breakfast and went out to find Huck.

Huck was sitting on the edge of a flatboat, his feet in the water. He looked very sad. Tom concluded to let Huck do the talking. If Huck didn't talk about the treasure, Tom would know it hadn't been real.

"Hello, Huck!"

"Hello yourself."

There was silence for a minute.

"Tom, if we'd have left the blamed tools at the dead tree, we'd have gotten that money! Oh, isn't it awful!"

"It isn't a dream, then! Somehow I almost wish it were. Doggoned if I don't, Huck."

"What isn't a dream?"

"Oh, that thing, yesterday. I've been half thinking it was."

"Dream! If the stairs hadn't broken down, you'd 'a' seen how much dream it was! I've had dreams all night, too—with that Spanish devil going for me all through 'em! Rot him!"

"No, not rot him. *Find* him. Track the money!"

"Tom, we'll never find him. We had one chance for such a pile—now that one's lost. I'd feel mighty shaky if I saw him, anyway!"

"Well, so would I. But, I'd like to see him, anyway—and track him down—to his Number Two."

"Number Two—yes, that's it! I've been thinking about that, but I can't make anything out of it. What do you think it is?"

"I don't know. It's too deep. Say, Huck, maybe it's the number of a house!"

"No, Tom, that isn't it. If it is, it isn't in this one-horse town!"

"Well, that's so. Let me think a minute. Here—it's the number of a room—in a tavern, you know!"

"Oh, that's the trick! There are only two taverns. We can find out quick!"

"You stay here, Huck, till I come back."

Tom was off at once. He was gone half an hour, but in that time he found that one of the taverns had No. 2 rented to a young lawyer, but the other one had a mystery about its No. 2. The tavern-keeper's young son said the room was kept locked all the time, and he never saw anybody go into it or come out of it except at night. He had noticed that there was a light in there the night before.

"That's what I found out, Huck. I guess that's the very No. 2 we're after!"

"I guess it is, Tom. Now what are you going to do?"

"Let me think."

Tom thought a long time. Then he said:

"I'll tell you. The back door of that No. 2 comes out into that little alley between the tavern and the old brick store. Now, you get hold of all the door keys you can find, and I'll take all of auntie's. The first dark night we'll go there and try 'em! And mind you, keep a lookout for Injun Joe, because he said he was going to drop into town and spy around once more for a chance to get his revenge. If you see him, follow him— if he doesn't go to that No. 2, that's not the place."

"Lordy, I don't want to follow him by myself!"

"Why, it'll be night, sure. He might never see you— and if he did, maybe he'd never think anything!"

"Well, if it's pretty dark I guess I'll track him. I don't know—I don't know. I'll try."

"You bet *I*'ll follow him, if it's dark, Huck! Why, he might have found out he couldn't get his revenge, and be going right after that money!"

"It's so, Tom, it's so. I'll follow him, I will, by jin-goes!"

"Now you're *talking*! Don't you ever weaken, Huck, and I won't!"

28 *Tom Enters Number Two*

That night Tom and Huck were ready for their adventure. They hung around the neighborhood of the tavern until after nine, one watching the alley at a distance and the other the tavern door. But the night didn't promise to be dark enough, so Tom went home. Huck watched for a time until twelve, then he retired to bed in his empty barrel.

Tuesday the boys had the same ill luck. Wednesday it was the same. But Thursday night promised a dark, black night. Tom slipped out with Aunt Polly's old tin lantern and a large cloth to hide the light with. He hid the lantern in Huck's barrel and the watch began.

An hour after midnight the tavern closed up and its lights were put out. No Spaniard had been seen. Nobody had entered or left the alley. Everything was right. The night was black and quiet. Only the sound of distant thunder could be heard.

Tom got his lantern, lit it in the barrel, and covered the light with the cloth. The two adventurers crept in the blackness toward the tavern. Then Huck stood watch while Tom felt his way into the alley.

Huck waited. Time passed slowly. Huck began to wish he could see a flash from the lantern to tell him that Tom was alive yet. It seemed hours since Tom had disappeared. Huck found himself drawing closer and closer to the alley in the hope he could hear, or see, something. Suddenly there was a flash of light and Tom came tearing by him.

"Run!" yelled Tom, "run for your life!"

Huck started making thirty or forty miles an hour at the first word. The boys never stopped running until they reached the shed of a deserted butchering house at the lower end of the village. Just as they got within its shelter the storm burst and the rain poured down. As soon as Tom got his breath, he said:

"Huck, it was awful! I tried two of the keys, just as soft as I could, but they made so much noise I could hardly get my breath, I was so scared. They wouldn't turn in the lock, either, but without noticing what I was doing, I turned the knob, and open came the door! It wasn't locked! I hopped in, took the cover off the light, and, *great Caesar's ghost!*"

"What—what did you see, Tom?"

"Huck, I almost stepped on Injun Joe's hand!"

"No!"

"Yes! He was lying there, sound asleep on the floor, with his old patch on his eye and his arms spread out!"

"Lordy! What did you do? Did he wake up?"

"No—never budged. Drunk, I guess. I just grabbed the lantern and started!"

"Say, Tom, did you see that box?"

"Huck, I didn't wait to look around. I didn't see the box, I didn't see the cross. I didn't see anything but a bottle and a tin cup on the floor by Injun Joe. Yes, and I saw two barrels and lots more whisky bottles in the room. The tavern keeps the whisky in that room."

"Who'd have thought such a thing? But say, Tom, now's a mighty good time to get that box, if Injun Joe's drunk."

"It is, that! You try it!"

Huck shuddered.

"Well, no—I guess not."

"And *I* guess not, Huck! Only one bottle alongside of Injun Joe isn't enough. If there'd been three, he'd be drunk enough, and I'd do it."

There was a long pause to think things over. Then Tom said:

"Look here, Huck, let's not try any more till we know Injun Joe's not in there. It's too risky. Now, if we watch every night, we'll be dead sure to see him go out, some time or other, and then we'll snatch that box quicker than lightning!"

"Well, I'm agreed. I'll watch the whole night long, and I'll do it every night, too, if you'll do the other part of the job."

"All right, I will. All you got to do is trot over and meow. If I'm asleep, you throw some gravel at the window. That'll wake me up."

"Agreed!"

"Now, Huck, the storm's over. I'll go home. It will be daylight in a couple of hours, but you go back and watch that long, will you?"

"I said I would, Tom, and I will! I'll haunt that tavern every night for a year! I'll sleep all day and I'll stand watch all night."

"That's fine. Now, where you going to sleep?"

"In Ben Rogers's hay barn. He lets me."

"Well, if I don't want you in the daytime, I'll let you sleep. Anytime you see something's up, in the night, just skip right around and meow!"

29 *Tom Picnics, but Huck—!*

The first thing Tom heard on Friday morning was the glad news that Judge Thatcher's family had come back to town. For a while Injun Joe and the treasure were forgotten as Tom spent his time with Becky and a crowd of their schoolmates. Later that day Becky teased her mother into letting her have her picnic the next day. Becky and Tom were delighted, and sent out invitations that same afternoon. Straightway the young people of the village were excitedly looking forward to the picnic.

That night, Tom's excitement kept him awake until a pretty late hour. He had good hopes of hearing Huck's "meow," and getting his treasure to surprise Becky and the picnickers with, next day. But, he was disappointed. No signal came that night.

Picnic time came, at last, and by ten o'clock a merry company were at Judge Thatcher's house, ready to start on the outing. The older people were not going along, for the children were considered safe enough under the wings of the older young people. The old steamboat was rented to take the gay crowd to the picnic spot down the river. Soon everyone was marching up the main street with picnic baskets. Sid was sick and had to miss the fun. Mary remained at home to entertain him. The last thing Mrs. Thatcher said to Becky was:

"You'll not get back till late. Perhaps you'd better stay all night with one of the girls that lives near the boat landing, child."

145

"Then I'll stay with Susy Harper, mamma."

"Very well. And mind, and behave yourself. Don't be any trouble!"

Presently, as they tripped along, Tom said to Becky:

"Say—I'll tell you what you can do—instead of staying at Susy Harper's, why not go right up the hill and stop at the Widow Douglas'? She'll have ice cream! She has it almost every day—loads of it! And she'll be awful glad to have you—and I'll stop for a while, too!"

"Oh, that will be fun!" Then Becky thought a moment, and added, "But what will mamma say?"

"How'll she ever know? Besides, what's the harm? All she wants is that you'll be safe. I bet she would have told you to go there if she'd have thought of it—I know she would!"

The Widow Douglas' friendliness and Tom's argument convinced Becky, but it was decided to say nothing to anybody about the night's program. Tom thought that maybe Huck might come that very night and give the signal, but Tom couldn't bear to give up the fun at Widow Douglas'. Anyway, Huck hadn't come the night before—maybe he wouldn't come this night, either. Tom decided not to think any more about it.

Three miles below town the steamboat stopped next to the picnic grounds and tied up. The crowd swarmed ashore and the picnic was underway. Then came the lunch, and a rest in the shade of the big oak trees after that. By and by somebody shouted:

"Who's ready for the cave?"

Everybody was. The cave was up the hillside, with the opening shaped like a letter A. Inside was a small chamber, chilly as an icehouse, and leading from that was a main avenue not more than eight or ten feet wide. Every few steps farther into the cave were more openings. These aisles ran into each other and out again and led nowhere. It was said that one might wander days and nights through the cave and never find the end of it. No one really knew the cave. Tom Sawyer had explored it as much as anyone.

Soon all were in the cave. Candles had been brought along to light the darkness. The moment a candle was lighted, someone knocked it down or blew it out. Then there were screams of laughter. By and by

everybody was hiding and surprising each other by jumping from hidden openings. Groups, and then couples, began to slip into the branch avenues. Sometimes they were able to hide from each other for half an hour.

At last one group after another came back to the mouth of the cave, panting, smeared with candle drippings and clay, but delighted with the success of the day. They were surprised to find that time had passed so quickly night was at hand. The steamship bell had been clanging for half an hour to call them. However, this made things more exciting, and when at last the steamboat pushed into the stream for home, nobody cared about the wasted time but the captain of the ship.

Huckleberry Finn was already upon his watch of the tavern when the boat's lights went blinking by. He heard no noise on board, for the young people were tired out from the picnic. He wondered what boat it was, but soon dropped it to put his attention upon his business.

A noise fell upon his ear. Huck was all attention in an instant. The alley door of the tavern closed softly. He sprang to the corner of the brick store. The next moment two men brushed by him. One seemed to have something under his arm. It must be the box! They were going to remove the treasure, Huck was sure. Why call Tom now—they would get away! Huck made up his mind to follow them.

They moved up the river street three blocks, then turned toward the big hill, found the path that led up, and took it. Halfway up the hill they passed the old Welshman's house. They climbed farther, never stopped at the stone pit, but went on up to the top of the hill. They plunged into the narrow path between the tall bushes, and were at once hidden in the blackness of the night.

Huck rushed along now, then slowed down, moved on a bit, and finally stopped to listen. There was no sound. At last an owl hooted, but he could hear no footsteps. Was everything lost?

Huck was about to spring forward, when a man cleared his throat not four feet from him! Huck's heart shot into his throat, but he swallowed it again. He stood there, shaking. But he knew where he was—he knew he was within five steps of a gate leading into the Widow Douglas' grounds. He thought, "Let them bury it there! It won't be hard to find."

Now there was a low voice, Injun Joe's:

"Damn her! She's got company—there's lights!"

"I can't see any." This was another voice—the stranger's, of the haunted house.

A deadly chill went to Huck's heart. This, then, was the revenge job! His first thought was to run, but then he remembered that the Widow Douglas had been kind to him more than once, and maybe these men were going to murder her! He wished he could warn her. Next he heard Injun Joe say:

"The bush is in your way. Now—this way—see?"

"Yes. There *is* company there. Better give it up."

"Give it up, and maybe never have another chance. I tell you again, I don't care for her money—but her husband was rough on me, many times! He was the justice of the peace that put me in jail for a tramp. And that's only a part of it—he had me *horsewhipped*— in front of the jail—with all the town looking on! HORSE- WHIPPED!—do you understand? He took advantage of me and died. But, I'll take it out on *her!*"

"Oh, don't kill her! Don't do that!"

"Who said anything about killing? I would kill *him* if he was here, but not her. When you want to get re- venge on a woman, you go for her face—cut her nose, slice her ears."

"But that's—"

"Keep your opinion to yourself! It'll be safest for you. I'll tie her to the bed. If she bleeds to death, is that my fault? My friend, you're going to help me, or I'll kill you! Do you understand that? And if I have to kill you, I'll kill her—then nobody will ever know much about this business!"

"Well, if it's got to be done, let's get at it—the quicker the better!"

"Do it *now*? And company there? Look here—what are you trying to do? No—we'll wait till the lights are out. There's no hurry."

Huck held his breath and stepped slowly backward. He put down his feet carefully, first one, then the other. He took several steps back, and then another, and another. Suddenly a twig snapped under his foot.

His breath stopped again. He listened. There was no sound. He turned, now, and then quickly, but care- fully, stepped along. When he came to the stone pit, he felt safe, and so he picked up his heels and fairly flew down the path until he reached the Welshman's. He banged at the door. Presently the heads of the old man and his two strong sons were at the windows.

"What's the matter? What do you want?"

"Let me in—quick!"

"Who are you?"

"Huckleberry Finn—quick, let me in!"

"Huckleberry Finn? All right—let him in lads, and let's see what's the trouble."

Huck told his story. Three minutes later the old man and his sons, all with guns, were up the hill. Huck went with them but stopped as they entered the brush near the fence. He hid behind a big rock and listened. There was a long, anxious silence. Then, all of a sudden, there were gunshots, and a cry!

Huck didn't want to find out what happened. He sprang away and sped down the hill as fast as his legs could carry him.

30 *Becky and Tom Disappear*

As soon as it was light on Sunday morning, Huck was back up the hill. He knocked gently at the old Welshman's door. Everyone inside was still asleep, but at last a call came from a window:

"Who's there?"

Huck answered in a low tone:

"Huck Finn!"

"Come in, lad—and welcome!"

The door was quickly unlocked, and Huck entered. He was given a seat while the old man and his two tall sons speedily dressed themselves.

"Now, my boy, I hope you're good and hungry, because breakfast will be ready soon. I and the boys hoped you'd turn up and stop here last night."

"I was awful scared," said Huck, "and I ran when the guns went off and I didn't stop for three miles! I've come back because I want to know about it, and I came early because I didn't want to run across those devils, even if they were dead!"

"No, they aren't dead, lad—we are sorry enough for that. You see, we knew right where to put our hands on them, as you told us. But, when we got within fifteen feet of them, I found I had to sneeze. I tried to keep it back, but it was no use. I was in the lead with my gun raised, and when the sneeze started, those villains ran. I yelled, 'Fire, boys!' and blazed away. So did the boys. I judge we never touched them. They fired back a shot apiece, but their bullets didn't do us any harm. We chased them, but lost them. Then we went down to tell the sheriff. He took some men and went off to guard the riverbank. As soon as it's light, the sheriff and some men are going to search the woods. My boys will join them presently. I wish we knew what those rascals looked like—it would help a good deal. You didn't see them, I suppose, in the dark, did you, lad?"

"Oh, yes, I saw them downtown, and followed them."

"Splendid! Describe them, my boy!"

"One's the old deaf and dumb Spaniard that's been around here once or twice, and the other is a mean-looking, ragged—"

"That's enough, lad, we know the men! We saw them in the woods back of the widow's house one day, and they sneaked away. Off with you, boys, and tell the sheriff!"

The Welshman's sons departed at once. As they were leaving the room, Huck sprang up and exclaimed:

"Oh, please don't tell *anybody* it was me that told on them! Please!"

"All right, if you say it, Huck. But, you ought to have the credit for what you did."

"Oh, no, no! Please don't tell!"

When the young men were gone, the old Welshman said:

"They won't tell—and I won't. But why don't you want it known?"

Huck would not explain much, further than to say he knew too much about one of those men and would not have the man know for fear the man would kill him for knowing. The old Welshman could see that Huck was hiding something, and said:

"My boy, don't be afraid of me. I wouldn't hurt a

hair of your head for all the world. No—I'd protect you. You know something about that Spaniard that you want to keep dark. Now trust me—tell me what it is— I won't give you away."

Huck looked into the old man's honest eyes a moment, then bent over and whispered:

"He isn't a Spaniard—he's Injun Joe!"

The Welshman almost jumped out of his chair. In a moment he said:

"It's all plain to me, now."

During breakfast the talk went on. The old man said that the last thing which he and his sons had done, before going to bed, was to get a lantern and go back to look around for marks of blood. They found none, but they did find—

"WHAT?"

Lightning could not have leaped faster than Huck asked. Had the Welshman and his sons found the treasure?

"Robber's tools. Why, what's the *matter* with you?"

Huck sank back, grateful—the treasure must still be in No. 2! If the men would be captured and jailed that day, he and Tom could seize the gold that night without any trouble. But Huck was ashamed he had nearly given the secret away.

Just as breakfast was completed there was a knock at the door. Huck jumped to hide. It was the Widow Douglas and several others who had heard the news. The Welshman told the story to the visitors. The Widow Douglas said she was grateful.

"Don't say a word about it, madam," said the Welshman. "There's another that you should be more thankful to than to me and my boys, but he won't allow me to tell his name. We wouldn't have been there but for him."

Then everybody wanted to know who it was, but the Welshman kept Huck's secret. The widow said:

"I went to sleep reading in bed and slept straight through all that noise. Why didn't you come and wake me?"

"We judged it wasn't worthwhile. We knew those fellows weren't likely to come back, and what was the use of waking you up and scaring you to death? Three men stood guard at your house all the rest of the night."

More visitors came, and the story had to be told and retold many times. Huck at last became so tired he went to sleep in a bed provided by the Welshman and slept through the rest of the day and all of the night.

At church, that same day, Judge Thatcher's wife saw Mrs. Harper and said to her:

"Is my Becky going to sleep all day? I thought she would be tired to death."

"Becky?"

"Yes." Mrs. Thatcher looked startled. "Didn't she stay with you last night?"

"Why, no."

Mrs. Thatcher turned pale, and sank into a seat, just as Aunt Polly came up and said:

"Good morning, Mrs. Thatcher. Good morning, Mrs. Harper. I've got a boy that's turned up missing. But, I suppose Tom stayed with one of you last night?"

Mrs. Thatcher shook her head, and turned paler than ever.

"He didn't stay with us!" said Mrs. Harper.

Now Aunt Polly looked worried. She turned to Joe Harper:

"Joe, have you seen my Tom this morning?"

"No'm."

"When did you see him last?"

Joe tried to remember, but wasn't sure he could

say. Other people were stopped, and children were asked. They all said they hadn't noticed if Tom and Becky were on the boat on the way back. It had been dark, and no one thought of asking if anyone were missing. One young man at last said that they might still be in the cave! Mrs. Thatcher fainted. Aunt Polly started to cry.

The alarm swept the town. Within five minutes bells were ringing and everyone was out looking for Becky and Tom. Before a half hour had gone by, two hundred men were on their way toward the cave.

All the long afternoon the village seemed empty and dead while the people searched. All the night long the town waited for news, but none came.

The old Welshman had joined the search, too. He came home toward daylight, almost worn out, and found Huck still in bed sick with fever and out of his head. The doctors were all at the cave, so the Widow Douglas came to look after Huck.

The search in the cave went on. Early in the forenoon parties of tired men came back to the village, but the strongest of the men continued searching. In one place of the cave the names "BECKY & TOM" were found traced on the wall. Near that place a bit of Becky's hair ribbon was discovered. But the children could not be found.

Three dreadful days and nights dragged by. The village sank into a hopeless fear. It cared for nothing. Even the closing of the tavern with No. 2 meant nothing to the town.

Huck got well enough to ask if anything had been discovered at the tavern since he had been ill.

"Yes," said the Widow.

Huck sat up in bed, worried:

"What—what was it?"

"Liquor!—and the place has been shut up. Lie down, child—what a scare you gave me!"

"Only tell me just one thing—only just one—please! Was it Tom Sawyer that found it?"

The Widow burst into tears. "Hush, hush, child," she said, "hush! I've told you before, you must *not* talk—you are very, very sick!"

Huck knew about the whisky. But why hadn't she mentioned the gold? Maybe the treasure was gone forever! But what could she be crying about? Huck didn't understand. He was still too weak to think things through and fell asleep.

The Widow said to herself, "There—he's asleep, poor boy. Tom Sawyer find it?—it's a pity but somebody could find Tom Sawyer! There are not many left, now, that've got hope enough, or strength enough, either, to go on searching!"

31 Lost, Found
—And Lost Again!

Now to return to Tom and Becky. They tripped along, during the picnic, to visit the cave, and were soon inside the dark aisles with the rest of the company. Presently the hide-and-seek game began, and Tom and Becky played it until it became tiresome. Then they wandered down a winding avenue, holding their candles high, and began to explore the cave.

They turned this way and that, drifting along and talking, and were soon far down into the secret depths of the cave. Tom wrote their names on a wall. Soon they came to a little stream, with a waterfall. Tom found a steep, natural stairway. This they followed until they came to what seemed a big room with many strange rock forms.

They went deeper into the cave. This brought them to a spring whose bottom glittered. Under the roof were thousands of bats. Disturbed by the light of the candles, the bats came flocking down by hundreds, screaming and darting at the lights. Tom took Becky's hand and ran with her from one passage to another until, at last, they escaped.

Tom found an underground lake, shortly, that was so big its shape was lost in the shadows. He wanted to explore it, but concluded that it would be best to sit down and rest awhile, first. Now, for the first time, they noticed how still it was. Becky said:

"Why, I didn't notice, but it seems ever so long since I heard any of the others!"

"Come to think of it, Becky, we are away down below them—I don't know how far! We couldn't hear them here."

Becky grew worried.

"I wonder how long we've been down here, Tom. We better start back!"

"Yes, I guess we better."

"Can you find the way, Tom? It's all twisted up to me."

"I guess I can find it. But those bats—if they put our candles out, we'll be in an awful fix. Let's try some other way, so as not to go through there!"

"Well—but I hope we won't get lost! It would be so awful!" Becky trembled at the thought.

They started to go back. They looked at every new opening they came to for familiar signs, but they were all strange. Then Tom shouted in the hope the others might hear him. There was no answer. He shouted again. There was no result.

Tom turned to Becky. "Becky," he said, "I can't find the way! It's all mixed up!"

"Tom, Tom, we're lost! We're lost! We never can get out of this awful place! Oh, why *did* we ever leave the others!"

She sank to the ground and burst out crying. Tom sat down by her and put his arms around her. She held fast to him, telling him how afraid she was. Tom said that it was all his fault for everything, but Becky replied he was no more to blame than she. She told him she would try to hope again and follow him wherever he might lead.

They moved on again. By and by Tom took Becky's candle and blew it out to save it. They grew tired but kept on moving. At last Becky's legs could carry her no farther. She sat down, Tom with her. They talked about home, and friends, then, until Becky grew so tired she fell asleep.

Tom was grateful as he saw how peaceful she looked. But Becky didn't sleep long. She woke, soon, and said:

"Oh, how *could* I sleep!"

"I'm glad you've slept, Becky. You'll feel rested, now, and we'll find the way out."

They rose up and wandered along, hand in hand. A long time after this Tom said they must find a spring. They found one presently, and Tom said it was time to rest again. Both were tired but Becky said she thought she could go on. Tom told her to sit down, took something out of his pocket, and said:

"Do you remember this?"

Becky almost smiled.

"It's our 'wedding cake', Tom!"

"Yes—I wish it were as big as a barrel, for it's all we've got!"

"I wanted to save it from the picnic for us to dream on, Tom, the way grown-up people do with wedding cake, but—"

She stopped. Tom divided the cake and both ate. They finished the feast with cold water from the spring. By and by Becky suggested that they move on again, but Tom said:

"Becky, can you bear it if I tell you something? We've got to stay here, where there's water to drink. That little piece is our last candle!"

Tears came to Becky again. Tom did what he could to comfort her, but it helped little, until Becky remembered something:

"Tom! They'll miss us and hunt for us!"

"Yes, they will. Certainly they will!"

"Maybe they're hunting for us now, Tom."

"Why, I guess maybe they are."

They fastened their eyes upon the last bit of candle and saw it melt slowly away. At last the light fluttered —and went out!

The darkness ruled. How long it was that Becky cried in Tom's arms neither could tell. All that they knew was that after what seemed a mighty stretch of time both awoke from a sleep. Tom said that it might be Sunday, now—maybe Monday—and, no doubt, the search was going on for them. He tried shouting, but the noise sounded so terrible that he stopped.

The hours wasted away. They became hungry again. Tom had saved a part of his cake. They divided and ate it, but the little food only made them seem hungrier.

Suddenly Tom said:

"*Sh!* Did you hear that?"

Both held their breath and listened. There was a sound like a shout, far off. Instantly Tom answered it, and, leading Becky by the hand, started feeling down the cave toward the noise. Presently he listened again. Again the sound came, this time a little nearer.

"They're coming!" said Tom. "Come along, Becky —we're all right now!"

Their speed was slow. Tom had to feel his way every step. At last they came to a spot Tom couldn't touch anything ahead. He said they must wait until the searchers came. They listened. This time the shoutings were farther away, and soon they could be heard no more. Then Tom yelled until he was hoarse. It was no use.

They felt their way back to the spring. The weary

time dragged on. They slept again, and awoke hungry and troubled. Tom believed it must be Tuesday by this time. But now an idea struck him. There were some side passages. He would explore them.

Tom took a kite string from his pocket and tied it to a stone. Then he and Becky started, unwinding the line as he searched along. At the end of twenty steps, the passage ended in space. Tom got down on his knees and felt as far as he could. He touched nothing. He tried to reach a little farther, and, at that moment, a man's hand, holding a candle, appeared from behind a rock not more than twenty yards below him!

Tom shouted. Instantly a man followed the hand —it was Injun Joe!

Tom couldn't move. He was vastly grateful the next moment to see Injun Joe turn and run out of sight. He wondered why Joe had not recognized his voice, but every noise in the cave sounded different. He was care-

ful to keep from Becky what he had seen. He told her he had only shouted for good luck.

They went back to the spring again. After another long wait, they fell asleep again. When they awoke, they were both raging with hunger. Tom believed it must be Wednesday or Thursday, now, or even Friday or Saturday. He felt sure the search had stopped.

He proposed to explore another passage, even if he ran into Injun Joe. But Becky was very weak. She could hardly move. She said she would wait, now, where she was. She told Tom to go with the kite line and explore, but she begged him to come back every little while and speak to her. She made him promise that if she should die, he would stay by her and hold her hand until all was over.

Tom kissed her, with a choking feeling in his throat. He told her he felt sure he would find the searchers or a way out of the cave. Then he took the kite string in his hand and went groping down one of the passages on his hands and knees, hungry, and unhappy with his gloomy fate.

32 Tom and Becky Are Found

In the village Tuesday afternoon came and drew toward nightfall. Everyone still grieved. The lost children had not been found. Public prayers had been offered up for them, but still no good news came from the cave. Most of the searchers had given up.

Mrs. Thatcher was very ill. She called Becky's name all the time. Aunt Polly was most sad. Her gray hair had grown almost white. The whole village went to rest that Tuesday night unhappy.

In the middle of the night, the bells of the village began to ring loudly. In a moment the streets were filled with people, who shouted, "They're found! They're found!" It was true. Becky and Tom, with a crowd of people around them, were being brought home.

The village lights went on. Nobody went to bed that night again. Everyone went to Judge Thatcher's house, where the children had been taken, to see the saved ones. Aunt Polly's happiness was complete, and Mrs. Thatcher's nearly so.

Tom lay upon a couch and told the story of the wonderful adventure. He finished by telling that he had left Becky and gone exploring by following the kite string as far as he could. He tried three times, in three directions, and was about to turn back the last time when he noticed a far-off spot that looked like daylight. He dropped the line and crawled toward the spot, pushed his head and shoulders through a small hole, and saw the broad river rolling by!

Tom told how lucky it was that it was daylight at the time. If it had been dark, he could not have seen the opening. He went back for Becky and helped her out of the cave. Both of them sat there and cried for gladness. A short time after, some men came along in a boat on the river and Tom called to them. He told the men about their situation and their hunger. At first, the men didn't believe his story—"Because," said they, "you are five miles down the river below the valley the cave is in!" But then they took Tom and Becky in the boat, rowed to a house, gave them supper, made them rest for several hours after dark, and then brought them home.

Before dawn, Judge Thatcher and a few other searchers with him still in the cave were called out and told of the great news.

Three days and nights of toil and hunger in the cave were hard on Tom and Becky, they soon found out. They were in bed for two days. Tom was up the next day, and downtown the day after that, nearly as whole as ever, but Becky didn't leave her room for three days.

Tom learned that Huck was sick and went to see him, but Huck was too weak to talk. Tom came to visit Huck every day after that, but the Widow Douglas told him not to excite Huck. She stayed with them to see that Tom obeyed. At home Tom learned that the Widow had been saved from harm, and that the other man with Injun Joe had been found in the river, drowned.

About two weeks later Huck was strong again. Tom started off to visit him and to tell him about the cave and the rescue. On the way, Tom passed Judge Thatcher's house. He stopped to see Becky. While he was there, the Judge and some friends got Tom to talking. Someone joked and asked Tom if he wouldn't like to go to the cave again. Tom said he thought he wouldn't mind. Then the Judge said:

"Well, Tom, there are others just like you, I've not the least doubt. But, we have taken care of that. Nobody will get lost in that cave any more!"

"Why?" Tom wanted to know.

"Because I had a big iron door put over the opening two weeks ago. The door is triple-locked—and I've got the keys!"

Tom turned as white as a sheet.

"What's the matter, boy! Here, run, somebody! Get a glass of water!"

The water was brought and thrown into Tom's face.

"Ah, now you're all right. What was the matter with you, Tom?"

"Oh, Judge, Injun Joe's in the cave!"

33 Three Surprises Meet Tom and Huck

Within a few minutes the news had spread that Injun Joe was in the cave, and a dozen boats filled with men were on their way to the cave. Even the steamboat, well filled with passengers, soon followed. Tom was in one of the small boats with Judge Thatcher.

When the cave door was unlocked, Injun Joe was found upon the ground, dead, with his face close to the crack of the door. Next to him was his big knife, its blade broken in two. He had tried to dig his way out, but failed, and had slowly starved to death. Tom felt sorry, but, at the same time, he felt safe now that Injun Joe was dead. Joe was buried near the mouth of the cave.

The morning after the funeral Tom took Huck to a private place to have an important talk. Huck had learned all about Tom's adventure in the cave by this time, but Tom hadn't heard all of Huck's story. After Huck had finished telling his entire adventure he said:

"Well, I guess the money is gone for us, Tom. It's not in No. 2."

"Huck, that money wasn't ever in No. 2!"

"What?" Huck searched his comrade's face keenly. "Tom, have you got on the track of that money again?"

"Huck, it's in the cave!"

Huck's eyes blazed.

"Honest, Tom?"

"Honest, Huck! Will you go in there with me and help get it out?"

"You bet I will—if it's where we can get to it and not get lost!"

"Huck, we can do that without the least little bit of trouble in the world."

"All right, if you say so. When do we go?"

"Right now, if you want to. Are you strong enough?"

"Is it far in the cave? I've been on my legs a little, now, but I can't walk more than a mile, Tom. At least, I don't think I could."

"It's about five miles, but there's a short cut only I know, Huck. I'll take you right to it, in a boat. You needn't even turn your hand over!"

"Let's start right away, Tom!"

"All right. We'll need some sandwiches, a little bag or two, two or three kite strings, and matches. I tell you, many's the time I wished I had some when I was in there before!"

A little after noon the boys borrowed a boat and got under way at once. When they were five miles below the mouth of the cave Tom said:

"See that white place up on the bluff? Well, that's one of my marks. We'll go ashore, now."

They landed.

"Now, Huck, where we are standing you could touch that hole I got out of with a fishing pole. See if you can find it."

Huck searched about, but found nothing. Then Tom marched proudly into a thick bush and said:

"Here it is! Look at it, Huck—it's the snuggest hole in this country! But you just keep mum about it. We've got it now, and we'll keep it quiet, only we'll let Joe Harper and Ben Rogers in."

Everything ready, the boys entered the hole, Tom in

the lead. As they went along they tied their kite strings together until their steps brought them to the spring. Tom trembled as he remembered his last experiences here. He showed Huck the place he and Becky had been when their last candle went out.

The boys began to whisper, now, for the stillness and gloom of the place troubled them. They went on, and presently reached the place that Tom had seen Injun Joe. But now the candles showed that it was not a big drop but only a steep clay hill twenty or thirty feet high. Tom whispered:

"Now I'll show you something, Huck!"

He held up his candle and then said:

"Look as far around the corner as you can. There —do you see that?"

"Tom, it's a *cross!*"

"*Now* where's your Number Two? '*Under the cross,*' hey? Right there's where I saw Injun Joe poke up his candle, Huck!"

Huck stared at the sign for a while, and then said with a shaky voice:

"Tom, let's get out of here!"

"What! and leave the treasure?"

"Yes, leave it! Injun Joe's ghost is around here, certain!"

"Look, Huck, Injun Joe's ghost isn't going to come around where there's a cross!"

Huck was convinced.

"Tom, I didn't think of that. But that's so. It's luck for us, that cross is. Let's climb down there and hunt for that box."

Tom went first, cutting steps in the clay hill. Four caves let out of the one in which the rock with the cross stood. Near the base of the rock they found some old blankets on which Joe had slept, but, there was no money box. The lads searched and searched, but found nothing. Tom said:

"He said *under* the cross. Well, this comes nearest to being under the cross. It can't be under the rock because that's solid on the ground."

They searched everywhere once more, without success. Huck could suggest nothing. By and by Tom said:

"Huck, there's footprints and some candle grease on the clay on one side of this rock, but not on the other side. Now, what's that for? I bet the money *is* under the rock! I'm going to dig in the clay."

Huck agreed. Tom's jackknife was out at once. He had not dug four inches before he struck wood.

"Hey, Huck!—do you hear that?"

Huck began to dig and scratch now. Some boards were soon uncovered and removed. They had hidden a natural cave which led under the rock. Tom got into the hole and held his candle ahead of him, but he couldn't see the end of the opening. He crawled ahead, then to the right, then to the left. Huck followed at his heels.

Tom turned a short curve, by and by, and exclaimed:

"My goodness, Huck, look here!"

It was the treasure box, sure enough! Next to it were an empty powder keg, a couple of guns in leather cases, two or three pairs of Indian moccasins, a leather belt, and a few other things.

"Got it at last!" said Huck. "My, but we're rich, Tom!"

"Huck, I always knew we'd get it. But, say—let's not fool around here. Let's get it out. Let me see if I can lift the box."

It weighed about fifty pounds. Tom could lift it, but it was too much work to carry it. The boys got the bags and the money was soon in them. They carried the bags to the cross rock.

"Now let's get the guns and things," said Huck.

"No, Huck—leave them there. They're just the things to have when we play robber. We'll keep them there all the time, and we'll hold our meetings there, too. But come along, Huck. We've been in here a long time. It's getting late, I guess, I'm hungry, too."

They presently came out into the clump of bushes, looked around, found the coast clear, and were soon lunching in the boat. As soon as the sun dipped in the west, they started rowing home. Tom skimmed up the shore, slowly, talking cheerily with Huck, and landed shortly after dark.

"Now, Huck," said Tom, "we'll hide the money in the loft of the widow's woodshed. I'll come up in the morning and we'll count it and divide it. Then we'll hunt up a place out in the woods for it where it will be safe. Just you wait here and watch the stuff till I run and get Benny Taylor's wagon. I won't be gone a minute."

He disappeared. Presently he returned with the wagon, put the sacks into it, threw some old rags on top of them, and started off. When the boys reached the Welshman's house, they stopped to rest. Just as they were about to move on, the Welshman stepped outside and said:

"Hello, who's that?"

"Huck, and Tom Sawyer."

"Good! Come along with me boys. You're keeping everybody waiting. Here—hurry up, walk ahead—I'll haul the wagon for you. My, it's heavy! Got bricks in it? Or old metal?"

"Old metal," said Tom.

"I thought so. The boys in this town will take more trouble to collect old iron to sell for junk! But, that's human nature. Hurry along, hurry along!"

The boys wanted to know what the hurry was about.

"Never mind. You'll see—when we get to the Widow Douglas'."

Huck said, with some fear:

"Mr. Jones, *we* haven't done anything!"

The Welshman laughed.

"Well, I don't know, Huck, my boy. I don't know about that. But aren't you and the widow good friends? What do you want to be afraid for?"

This question wasn't entirely answered before Mr. Jones left the wagon near the door of the widow's house and pushed the boys inside one of the big rooms. The place was grandly lighted and everybody of importance in the village was there. The Thatchers were there, the Harpers, Aunt Polly, Sid, Mary, and a great many more, and all dressed in their best. Mr. Jones turned to the people and said:

"Tom wasn't at home, yet, so I gave him up, but, I stumbled on him and Huck right at my door! I just brought them along in a hurry."

"And you did just right!" said the widow. "Come with me, boys."

She took them to a bedroom and said:

"Now wash and dress yourselves. Here are two new suits of clothes for you—shirts, socks, everything complete—they'll fit both of you. Get into them. We'll wait—come down when you're dressed."

Then she left.

34 More Surprises Await —Everyone

Huck said:

"Tom, we can skip out, if we can find a rope. The window isn't high from the ground!"

"Shucks, what do you want to sneak out for?"

"Well, I'm not used to that kind of a crowd. I can't stand it. I'm not going down there, Tom."

"Oh, it's nothing. I don't mind it a bit. I'll take care of you."

Sid appeared.

"Tom," said he, "auntie has been waiting for you all afternoon. Mary got your good clothes ready, and everybody's been worrying where you were. Say—isn't this candle grease and clay, on your clothes?"

"Now, Mr. Siddy, you just 'tend to your own business! What's this big party for anyway?"

"It's one of the widow's parties that she's always having. This time it's for the Welshman and his sons for saving her the other night. And say—I can tell you something, if you want to know!"

"Well, what?"

"Why, old Mr. Jones is going to try to spring something on the people here tonight as a secret, but I heard him tell auntie. I guess it's not much of a secret now. Mr. Jones was bound Huck should be here—couldn't get along with his grand old secret without Huck, you know!"

"Secret about what, Sid?"

"About Huck tracking the robbers to the widow's.

I guess Mr. Jones was going to make a grand time over his surprise, but I bet it will drop pretty flat!"

Sid laughed in a very contented and satisfied way.

"Sid, was it you that told?"

"Oh, never mind who it was. *Somebody* told—that's enough."

"Sid, you're a mean little kid! If you had been in Huck's place you'd have sneaked down the hill and never told anybody on the robbers!" Tom cuffed Sid's ears and pushed him toward the door. "Now go and tell auntie, if you dare!"

Some minutes later the boys were downstairs and at the supper table. Mr. Jones made his speech and told his secret about Huck's share in the adventure. The widow thanked Huck so much that he nearly forgot about the trouble his new clothes were giving him. She said she meant to have Huck live with her and go to school, and when he finished school and she could spare the money, she would start him in a business.

Tom's chance was come. He said:

"Huck doesn't need money. Huck's rich!"

The company tried to be polite and not laugh, even though this seemed to be a joke. There was silence. Tom broke it:

"Huck's got money. Maybe you don't believe it, but he's got lots of it! Oh, you needn't smile—I guess I can show you. You just wait a minute!"

Tom ran out of doors. The company looked at each other—and then at Huck. But Huck didn't say a word.

"Sid, what ails Tom?" asked Aunt Polly. "He—well, there isn't ever any making out of that boy! I never—"

Tom entered, struggling with the weight of the sacks, and Aunt Polly did not finish her sentence. Tom poured the mass of yellow coins upon the table and said:

"There—what did I tell you? Half of it's Huck's and half of it is mine!"

This took everybody's breath away. All gazed, nobody spoke for a moment. Then everyone wanted to know about the money. Tom explained. The tale was long but full of interest, for no one stopped him. When he had finished, Mr. Jones said:

"I thought I had fixed up a little surprise for this occasion, but it doesn't amount to anything, now! This one makes it seem mighty small, I'm willing to admit!"

The money was counted. The sum amounted to a little over twelve thousand dollars. It was more money than anyone there had seen at one time!

35 The Adventures End —With Plans for More

Tom and Huck now became heroes. They were admired and stared at. Everybody wanted their company. Their unexpected piece of good luck in finding the money sent everyone in the little village treasure hunting. People looked in every old house for money and dug holes everywhere. The boys became so famous newspapers printed stories of their lives.

The Widow Douglas put Huck's money in the bank, and Judge Thatcher did the same with Tom's at Aunt Polly's request. Each lad had an income, now, from the interest the money drew at the bank.

Judge Thatcher liked Tom more and more. He said that no ordinary boy would ever have gotten his daughter out of the cave. When Becky told her father how Tom had taken her whipping for her at school, the Judge said Tom had done a noble thing, and that he hoped to see Tom a great lawyer or a great soldier some day. The Judge said he would look to it to see that Tom got the best training in order to be ready for either career.

Huck Finn's wealth and the fact that he was now living with the Widow Douglas introduced him into society—no, dragged him into it. It was almost more than he could stand. He had to wash, and comb and brush his hair. He had to eat with knife and fork and use napkin, cup, and plate. He had to learn books and go to church. He had to speak just so. No matter which way he turned, he had to do things right.

Huck bravely bore this life for three weeks, and then, one day, he was missing. The widow looked for him but couldn't find him. At last Tom found him, three days later, in an old empty barrel. Huck had slept there and was living there in his old way. He hadn't washed, his hair was uncombed. He had on his old clothes, but he was free and happy.

Tom called him out of the barrel and told him the trouble he was causing with everybody looking for him. Tom urged him to go home. Huck's face lost its happy look and took on a sad expression. He said:

"Don't talk about it, Tom. I've tried it, and it doesn't work! It's not for me. I'm not used to it. The widow's good to me, and friendly, but I can't stand getting up every morning and washing and combing my hair and wearing those new clothes. Those clothes choke me, Tom! They don't seem to let any air get through them, somehow, and they're so nice and clean I can't sit down or roll around anywheres! Besides, I've got to wear shoes! The widow eats by a bell, goes to bed by a bell, and gets up by a bell. Everything is so awful regular I can't stand it!"

"But everybody does it that way, Huck!"

"Tom, it doesn't make any difference. I'm not everybody, and I can't *stand* it! It's awful to be tied up so. All I want to do is go fishing and swimming, but there I got to ask to do everything, and the widow wouldn't let me yell, nor stretch, nor scratch before folks, nor anything! Besides, school's going to open, and I'd have to go to it—well, I couldn't stand *that*, Tom!"

Huck went on:

"Looky-here, Tom, being rich isn't what it's cracked up to be. It's just worry and work all the time! Now, these clothes suit me, and this barrel suits me, and

I'm going to stick to 'em. Tom, I wouldn't ever have gotten into all this trouble if it hadn't been for that money! Now, you just take my share of it, and give me a dime now and then—not many times, because I don't care for a thing unless it's hard to get. Now you go and tell the widow for me."

"Oh, Huck, you know I can't do that! It isn't fair. Besides, if you'll try this thing just a while longer, you'll come to like it!"

"Like it! Yes—the way I'd like a hot stove if I had to sit on it long enough. No, Tom, I won't be rich, and I won't live in those choky houses. I like the woods, and the river, and barrels, and I'll stick to 'em, too. Blame it all! Just as we'd gotten guns, and a cave, and all just fixed up to play robbers, this foolishness has got to come up and spoil it all!"

Tom saw his opportunity—

"Looky-here, Huck, being rich isn't going to keep me back from turning robber!"

"No? Oh, are you dead sure, Tom?"

"Just as dead sure as I'm sitting here! But Huck, we can't let you into the gang if you aren't respectable, you know."

"Can't let me in, Tom? Didn't you let me go as a pirate?"

Huck's joy was ended.

"Yes, but that's different. A robber is more high-toned than what a pirate is—as a general thing."

"Now, Tom, haven't you always been friendly to me? You wouldn't shut me out, would you, Tom? You wouldn't do that, now, *would* you, Tom?"

"Huck, I wouldn't want to, and I *don't* want to. But, what would people say? Why, they'd say, 'Humph! Tom Sawyer's Gang! Pretty low characters in it!' And they'd mean you, Huck! You wouldn't like that, and I wouldn't."

Huck was silent for some time, struggling with himself. Finally he said:

"Well, I'll go back to the widow for a month and tackle it and see if I can come to stand it—if you'll let me belong to the gang, Tom."

"All right, Huck, it's agreed! Come along, old chap, and I'll ask the widow to let up on you a little, Huck."

"Will you, Tom? Now, will you? That's good—if she'll let up on some of the roughest things. When are you going to start the gang and turn robbers?"

"Oh, right away. We'll get the boys together and start tonight, maybe."

"Now, that's something! Why, this will be a million times better than pirating. I'll stick to the widow till I rot, Tom, and if I get to be a regular ripper of a robber, and everybody talking about it, I guess she'll be proud she took me in!"

Conclusion

So ends this story. Since it is only a history of a *boy*, it must stop here. The story could not go much further without becoming the history of a *man*. When one writes a novel about grown people, he knows exactly where to stop—that is, with a marriage. But, when one writes of young people, he must stop where he best can.

REVIEWING YOUR READING

CHAPTER 1

FINDING THE MAIN IDEA

1. The purpose of this chapter is to tell that
   (A) a new boy came to town   (B) Tom always got into trouble   (C) Tom didn't like school   (D) Aunt Polly often punished Tom

REMEMBERING DETAILS

2. Where did Tom hide from his aunt?
   (A) Under the bed   (B) In the closet   (C) Behind the fence   (D) In the backyard
3. Tom avoided being beaten for eating the jam by
   (A) apologizing to his aunt   (B) buying new jam
   (C) hiding from his aunt   (D) blaming Sid
4. Aunt Polly thought that Tom skipped school in order to
   (A) sleep   (B) fight   (C) play with the water pump
   (D) swim in the river

DRAWING CONCLUSIONS

5. You can figure out that Tom's collar was sewn with a different-colored thread because Tom
   (A) sewed it himself   (B) ripped it in a fight   (C) changed his shirt   (D) wore a new shirt

USING YOUR REASON

6. When the author says that the new boy wore shoes on Friday, he means that the boy was
   (A) tall   (B) wealthy   (C) happy   (D) fat
7. Aunt Polly wanted to punish Tom because she
   (A) was angry at him   (B) disliked him   (C) didn't want to spoil him   (D) liked Sid better

IDENTIFYING THE MOOD

8. Tom's attitude toward life was
   (A) carefree   (B) serious   (C) fearful   (D) hostile

READING FOR DEEPER MEANING

9. What quality do you think the author admires most in Tom?
   (A) Honesty   (B) Bravery   (C) Adventurousness
   (D) Kindness

THINKING IT OVER

1. What do you think the author's opinion of Sid was? Do you think Aunt Polly preferred him to Tom? Do you like Sid? Explain your opinion of Sid.
2. What does the fight scene tell you about Tom? What does it tell you about the boys in the village? Do you think they were mean and unfriendly? Why or why not?

CHAPTER 2

FINDING THE MAIN IDEA

1. This chapter is mostly about how Tom
   (A) annoys Sid   (B) gets out of work   (C) makes new friends   (D) learns to paint

REMEMBERING DETAILS

2. When did Tom have to whitewash the fence?
   (A) After school   (B) On Saturday   (C) On Sunday morning   (D) After dinner
3. Tom got Ben to help him whitewash by
   (A) pretending it was fun   (B) paying him   (C) doing a bad job   (D) beating him
4. Tom's great law of human action is that people want something if it is
   (A) free   (B) valuable   (C) hard to get   (D) new and shiny
5. Tom was rolling in wealth at the end of the day because
   (A) many boys paid him   (B) Aunt Polly paid him
   (C) he found some money   (D) he sold the paint

DRAWING CONCLUSIONS

6. Aunt Polly didn't want Jim to help Tom because
   (A) she paid Tom to whitewash   (B) Jim would do a bad job   (C) Tom liked to work alone   (D) she was punishing Tom

USING YOUR REASON

7. Tom didn't want the boys to see him whitewash because they would

   (A) make fun of him   (B) want to help   (C) tell their teacher   (D) throw mud at the fence

IDENTIFYING THE MOOD

8. When Tom wanted a person to believe something, he could be very

   (A) truthful   (B) convincing   (C) insistent   (D) polite

READING FOR DEEPER MEANING

9. This chapter suggests that when faced with an unpleasant job, you should

   (A) make the best of it   (B) try to get out of it   (C) do your fair share   (D) grin and bear it

10. The author would probably agree that people

    (A) can see through most tricks   (B) like to help others
    (C) like to work hard   (D) can be fooled easily

THINKING IT OVER

1. Do you agree with Tom's great law of human action? Why or why not?

2. Irony can mean "a situation that is opposite of what you'd expect." Give some examples of irony in this chapter. How do these situations differ from what you had expected?

CHAPTER 3

FINDING THE MAIN IDEA

1. This chapter is mostly about

   (A) Aunt Polly's injustice   (B) Sid's dishonesty and tricks
   (C) Tom's love and sorrow   (D) Tom's war games

REMEMBERING DETAILS

2. Tom got even with Sid for

   (A) stealing his apple   (B) breaking the sugar bowl
   (C) not whitewashing   (D) telling about the black thread

3. Tom went to the village square to

   (A) go to school   (B) play war   (C) meet the new girl
   (D) go to the post office

4. Who was Amy Lawrence?
   (A) Tom's old girl friend   (B) Tom's cousin   (C) Tom's new girl friend   (D) Tom's Sunday School teacher
5. What did Tom do to attract the new girl's attention?
   (A) Wrote her a letter   (B) Asked her for a date
   (C) Gave her a flower   (D) Showed off
6. Who broke the sugar bowl?
   (A) Sid   (B) Tom   (C) Mary   (D) Aunt Polly

USING YOUR REASON

7. When the author refers to Tom's "pleasant sufferings," he means that Tom
   (A) tried to cheer up   (B) liked to hurt others
   (C) enjoyed feeling sorry for himself   (D) made everyone laugh

IDENTIFYING THE MOOD

8. The author probably feels that Tom's sorrow was
   (A) slightly funny   (B) tragic   (C) unending
   (C) unbearable

THINKING IT OVER

1. Both Tom and Sid stole some sugar, but Sid let Tom take the blame both times. How is Sid's character different from Tom's?
2. This chapter tells how Tom's imagination worked when he felt bad. Do you think people often feel the way Tom did? Explain your answer.

CHAPTER 4

FINDING THE MAIN IDEA

1. This chapter is mostly about
   (A) Tom's tricks in Sunday School   (B) Mary's visit
   (C) Tom's lesson   (D) Sid's new Bible

REMEMBERING DETAILS

2. What did Tom have to do for Sunday School?
   (A) Learn a hymn   (B) Make a sermon   (C) Write a report   (D) Recite verses
3. Mary gave Tom a new
   (A) knife   (B) Bible   (C) kite   (D) pair of shoes

4. Tom got his tickets by
   (A) trading   (B) stealing   (C) winning them
   (D) buying them

USING YOUR REASON

5. When the author said it would be kind to "draw the curtain over the rest of the scene," he meant that it was
   (A) boring   (B) embarrassing   (C) finished
   (D) forgotten

DRAWING CONCLUSIONS

6. You can figure out that Tom felt bad when he couldn't name the disciples because
   (A) he was afraid of the teacher   (B) he wanted the Bible badly   (C) the new girl was watching   (D) Sid would tell Aunt Polly

THINKING IT OVER

1. The author says that when the Judge came to Sunday School, "soon everyone was showing off." What does this tell you about the author's opinion of human nature?
2. How does the author make fun of the Sunday School teacher? Give examples.

CHAPTER 5

FINDING THE MAIN IDEA

1. In this chapter, the author is mostly interested in
   (A) Tom's treasures   (B) Sunday School   (C) a church service   (D) Tom's new dog

REMEMBERING DETAILS

2. Tom sat next to the aisle so he
   (A) could hear better   (B) could leave early   (C) could help the minister   (D) couldn't look out the window
3. Why didn't the boys like Willie Mufferson?
   (A) He was too stupid.   (B) He was too good.   (C) He was a thief.   (D) He was a liar.
4. Tom's treasure was a
   (A) beetle   (B) dog   (C) knife   (D) Bible
5. The dog yelped because
   (A) Tom pulled his tail   (B) he saw a cat   (C) a beetle bit him   (D) the minister chased him

DRAWING CONCLUSIONS

6. Some people felt "an inward joy" when the dog yelped because they

   (A) hated dogs   (B) were bored with the sermon
   (C) liked the minister's jokes   (D) were fond of Tom

READING FOR DEEPER MEANING

7. This chapter suggests that laughter

   (A) doesn't belong in church   (B) can be cruel   (C) can be refreshing   (D) can be foolish

THINKING IT OVER

1. A *satire* is a type of writing that makes us laugh at foolishness or dishonesty. Find examples in this chapter that show *Tom Sawyer* is a satire. Tell what the author thinks is foolish or dishonest.

2. Do you think most people secretly feel the way Tom does about school and church and proper clothes? Explain your answer.

CHAPTER 6

REMEMBERING DETAILS

1. Tom pretended his toe was dead in order to

   (A) miss school   (B) go to the hospital   (C) make Becky feel bad   (D) scare Sid

2. Aunt Polly pulled Tom's tooth out with

   (A) her fingers   (B) a pair of pliers   (C) thread and a chunk of fire   (D) thread and a doorknob

3. The town treated Huck Finn like

   (A) a hero   (B) a friend   (C) a relative   (D) an outcast

4. What did Huck think a dead cat was good for?

   (A) Curing warts   (B) Scaring people   (C) Curing measles   (D) Killing mice

DRAWING CONCLUSIONS

5. You can figure out that Tom probably envied Huck because Huck

   (A) was older   (B) was rich   (C) could whistle through his teeth   (D) could do as he pleased

6. Mother Hopkins was probably

   (A) a doctor   (B) a ghost   (C) a real witch   (D) an old woman

USING YOUR REASON

7. Tom deliberately told the teacher that he talked to Huck in order to
   (A) sit next to Becky   (B) show he wasn't ashamed
   (C) get sent home   (D) make everyone laugh

THINKING IT OVER

1. Huck and Tom believed in magic and witchcraft. Today, many people believe in superstitions, such as the one that says black cats are bad luck. Do you know anyone who has a superstition? How do you think the superstition affects the person?

CHAPTER 7

FINDING THE MAIN IDEA

1. This chapter is mostly about
   (A) Tom's friend Joe   (B) Tom's new love   (C) Becky's drawing   (D) lunch hour

REMEMBERING DETAILS

2. In school, Tom and Joe play with
   (A) a deck of cards   (B) jacks   (C) a dog   (D) a tick
3. When did Tom meet Becky?
   (A) After school   (B) During lunch hour   (C) Over the weekend   (D) After supper
4. Tom wanted Becky to
   (A) become engaged to him   (B) give him a cat   (C) help him with his lessons   (D) play ball with him
5. What did Tom do when Becky wouldn't stop crying?
   (A) Hit her   (B) Apologized   (C) Played hookey
   (D) Found another girl friend

DRAWING CONCLUSIONS

6. If the other students had known that Becky was meeting Tom, they probably would have
   (A) told the teacher   (B) teased Tom and Becky   (C) told Aunt Polly   (D) left them alone

USING YOUR REASON

7. Becky became upset because Tom
   (A) argued with her   (B) tried to steal her chewing gum
   (C) had an old girl friend   (D) tripped her

THINKING IT OVER

1. When Tom offered Becky his most prized possession, a brass doorknob, she rejected it. How do you think Tom felt? Have you ever had a similar experience? Describe how you felt.

CHAPTER 8

FINDING THE MAIN IDEA

1. This chapter is mostly about how Tom
   (A) fights with Becky   (B) plays hookey   (C) gets sick
   (D) stays after school

REMEMBERING DETAILS

2. When he ran away, Tom finally decided to be a
   (A) sailor   (B) doctor   (C) pirate   (D) soldier
3. Tom thought you could find lost marbles with a
   (A) magnet   (B) compass   (C) trained dog   (D) magic spell
4. What did Tom and Joe Harper play?
   (A) Cowboys and Indians   (B) Soldiers   (C) Robin Hood
   (D) Hide-and-seek

DRAWING CONCLUSIONS

5. You can figure out from this chapter that when Tom played he liked to be
   (A) a follower   (B) an observer   (C) a leader   (D) a peacemaker

USING YOUR REASON

6. Tom wanted to run away in order to
   (A) make Becky suffer   (B) quit school   (C) support his family   (D) meet new people

IDENTIFYING THE MOOD

7. You can tell from this chapter that Tom's mood was always
   (A) sad   (B) happy   (C) changing   (D) the same

THINKING IT OVER

1. Tom and Joe had trouble studying in school but they could memorize the whole book of Robin Hood. Where do you think they learned the most—in or out of school? What do you think the author feels about playing and imagination? Are they important? Explain your answer.

CHAPTER 9

FINDING THE MAIN IDEA

1. This chapter is mostly about
   (A) curing warts (B) a murder in a graveyard (C) the ghost of Hoss Williams (D) Injun Joe's past

REMEMBERING DETAILS

2. Why wouldn't Tom fall asleep?
   (A) He was waiting for Huck. (B) Aunt Polly was snoring. (C) Sid tossed in bed. (D) He wasn't tired.
3. Huck and Tom signaled each other by
   (A) whistling (B) meowing (C) humming (D) barking
4. When three figures appeared in the graveyard, Huck first thought they were
   (A) ghosts (B) thieves (C) Indians (D) devils
5. Who killed the doctor?
   (A) Potter (B) Injun Joe (C) The sheriff (D) Huck's father
6. When did the boys run away?
   (A) Before Joe and Potter dug up the body (B) After the stabbing (C) After Joe and Potter left the scene
   (D) Before the murder

DRAWING CONCLUSIONS

7. You can figure out that the doctor probably wanted the body for
   (A) revenge (B) experiments (C) money (D) a practical joke

USING YOUR REASON

8. Injun Joe blamed the doctor for
   (A) killing his father (B) sending him to jail (C) giving him fake medicine (D) stealing his money
9. Potter was confused about the murder because he had
   (A) lost his memory (B) drunk too much (C) gone crazy (D) run away

IDENTIFYING THE MOOD

10. After the murder, Potter felt
    (A) relieved (B) hopeful (C) horrified (D) violent

THINKING IT OVER

1. Why do you think Injun Joe was especially feared by Huck and Tom?
2. Grave robbing was not as unusual in Tom's day as it would be today. Why do you think this was so?

CHAPTER 10

FINDING THE MAIN IDEA

1. In this chapter, the author is mostly concerned with
(A) what Potter did after the murder (B) how Injun Joe escaped (C) what Tom and Huck did after the murder (D) how Sid found out about Tom

REMEMBERING DETAILS

2. Why wouldn't the boys tell about the murder?
(A) They wanted to frame Potter. (B) They were afraid they would be blamed. (C) They were afraid they would be killed. (D) They weren't sure about what had happened.
3. The boys took an oath to
(A) get Injun Joe (B) help Potter (C) run away (D) keep silent
4. Who was sleeping in the tannery?
(A) Muff Potter (B) Huck's father (C) Injun Joe (D) Jim
5. How did Aunt Polly make Tom feel bad?
(A) She wept. (B) She beat him. (C) She wouldn't speak to him. (D) She wouldn't give him his breakfast.

DRAWING CONCLUSIONS

6. To Tom and Huck, the howling of a stray dog meant
(A) the dog was lost (B) someone would die (C) someone had died (D) the dog was sick
7. Who told Aunt Polly that Tom had been out all night?
(A) Mary (B) Sid (C) Tom (D) Muff

USING YOUR REASON

8. Instead of saying Muff was a "goner," Tom could have said that Muff was
(A) asleep (B) running away (C) going to die (D) drunk

THINKING IT OVER

1. Why did Tom and Huck decide to give up their "evil" ways in this chapter? Do you think they really will change their ways? Why or why not?

2. Do you think the boys were right not to tell about the murder? Why or why not?

CHAPTER 11

FINDING THE MAIN IDEA

1. This chapter is mostly about
(A) Tom's confession   (B) Joe's hanging   (C) Muff's arrest   (D) Tom's sleeplessness

REMEMBERING DETAILS

2. When they heard of the murder most of the townspeople went to the
(A) village square   (B) graveyard   (C) jail   (D) church

3. Who did the knife belong to?
(A) Huck's father   (B) Injun Joe   (C) Muff Potter
(D) Doctor Robinson

4. The boys thought Injun Joe had sold himself to the devil because Joe
(A) got away with his lie   (B) never grew old   (C) had superhuman strength   (D) looked like the devil

USING YOUR REASON

5. Muff went back to the graveyard in order to
(A) look at the body   (B) give himself up   (C) bury the body   (D) get the knife

IDENTIFYING THE MOOD

6. How did Tom feel about Muff's arrest?
(A) Glad   (B) Doubtful   (C) Amused   (D) Disturbed

7. The townspeople felt that Injun Joe was
(A) admirable   (B) frightening   (C) ridiculous
(D) ignorant

READING FOR DEEPER MEANING

8. The author would probably agree that crowds of people
(A) don't always make good decisions   (B) can always recognize the truth   (C) never get excited   (D) always act like wild animals

THINKING IT OVER

1. How is Tom's village different from today's towns and cities?
2. Do you think the village enjoyed the excitement of the murder and arrest? Explain your answer.

CHAPTER 12

FINDING THE MAIN IDEA

1. This chapter is mostly about how
(A) Muff liked prison   (B) Tom missed Becky   (C) Aunt Polly cured Tom   (D) Becky teased Tom

REMEMBERING DETAILS

2. Becky stopped coming to school because she
(A) moved   (B) played hookey   (C) visited her aunt
(D) became ill
3. Tom suddenly felt better because
(A) Becky came back to school   (B) he hated his Aunt's medicine   (C) he ate better   (D) he took the water treatment
4. Who did Tom give the Pain-killer to?
(A) Sid (B) Aunt Polly   (C) The cat   (D) Becky
5. Why did Tom's heart break again?
(A) Becky was mean to him.   (B) Becky died.   (C) Becky found a new boyfriend.   (D) Becky moved away.

USING YOUR REASON

6. Tom told the boys he was sick because he didn't want them to know that
(A) he longed for Becky   (B) Injun Joe frightened him
(C) he couldn't play their games   (D) Aunt Polly was punishing him

IDENTIFYING THE MOOD

7. Tom felt bad because
(A) he caught a cold   (B) Muff was arrested   (C) Becky stopped coming to school   (D) Huck ran away

READING FOR DEEPER MEANING

8. The author would probably agree that grown-ups
(A) always do the right thing   (B) always make life miserable for young people   (C) sometimes don't think of young people's feelings   (D) never change their ways

194

THINKING IT OVER

1. Aunt Polly's cures for Tom's illness are examples of folk medicine. Do you know any examples of folk medicines that are used today? Do you think these cures really work? Explain your answers.

CHAPTER 13

FINDING THE MAIN IDEA

1. In this chapter the author mostly tells about
   (A) working in school   (B) running away   (C) building a raft   (D) stealing a boat

REMEMBERING DETAILS

2. Tom decided to become a pirate because he thought
   (A) school was boring   (B) no one loved him   (C) pirates made lots of money   (D) the sea was safe
3. Who was also running away?
   (A) Sid   (B) Jeff Thatcher   (C) Mary   (D) Joe Harper
4. Where did the pirates get their food?
   (A) They grew it.   (B) They worked for it.   (C) They stole it.   (D) They bought it.

DRAWING CONCLUSIONS

5. You can figure out that the boys got most of their ideas about pirates from
   (A) adventure stories   (B) friends who were pirates
   (C) their own imaginations   (D) their teachers

USING YOUR REASON

6. Instead of calling them "queer pirates" the author could have called them
   (A) foreign pirates   (B) terrible pirates   (C) crazy pirates
   (D) make-believe pirates

THINKING IT OVER

1. One of the reasons that *Tom Sawyer* is so popular is because Tom wants to do things that many people want to do—like run away and have exciting adventures. Do you ever imagine having adventures like Tom's? Tell about them.
2. Do you think Tom and Joe are serious about running away? Why do you think so?

CHAPTER 14

FINDING THE MAIN IDEA

1. In this chapter, the author is mostly concerned with how the boys
   (A) got food   (B) explored the island   (C) felt about their adventure   (D) tricked the search party

REMEMBERING DETAILS

2. What did the boys eat for breakfast?
   (A) Eggs   (B) Cereal   (C) Fish   (D) Ham
3. How did the boys feel after a full day on the island?
   (A) Scared   (B) Happy   (C) Tired   (D) Homesick
4. What were the people on the steamboat searching for?
   (A) Injun Joe   (B) A stolen boat   (C) The bodies of the boys   (D) Muff Potter
5. The boys felt like heroes because they were
   (A) outlaws   (B) brave   (C) the center of attention
   (D) the terror of the whole village

DRAWING CONCLUSIONS

6. You can figure out at the end of this chapter that Tom was probably going
   (A) swimming   (B) away   (C) home   (D) hunting

USING YOUR REASON

7. Tom poked fun at Joe for feeling homesick because he didn't
   (A) feel the same way   (B) want Huck to feel left out
   (C) want to show that he was also homesick   (D) like Joe

THINKING IT OVER

1. How would you feel if you lived on an island like the one in the story? Would you get bored? Would you enjoy yourself? Would you get homesick? Explain your answers.

CHAPTER 15

FINDING THE MAIN IDEA

1. This chapter is mostly concerned with
   (A) Tom's funeral   (B) Tom's visit home   (C) Aunt Polly's search party   (D) Mrs. Harper's news

REMEMBERING DETAILS

2. Tom heard Aunt Polly's conversation because he was hidden
(A) in the backyard   (B) outside the window   (C) in the
bedroom   (D) under the couch

3. Aunt Polly felt that Tom was
(A) better off dead   (B) full of life   (C) thoroughly bad
(D) very unlucky

4. When would the boys' funerals be held?
(A) The next day   (B) Sunday morning   (C) Next week
(D) That afternoon

5. Why didn't Tom tell everyone he was alive?
(A) He was afraid he'd be punished.   (B) He had too much
fun listening.   (C) He didn't want to scare anyone.
(D) He never wanted to come back.

6. When Aunt Polly was asleep Tom went to
(A) steal some money   (B) wake her up   (C) kiss her
(D) leave a note

USING YOUR REASON

7. Tom didn't keep the boat he borrowed because he
(A) knew people would look for it   (B) gave up stealing
(C) lost it   (D) couldn't row it

THINKING IT OVER

1. Do you think it was wrong of Tom not to tell anyone he was
alive? Why or why not? Would you have done the same thing
if you were Tom? Explain your answer.

CHAPTER 16

FINDING THE MAIN IDEA

1. Which of the following is the best title for this chapter?
(A) "Good-bye, Island"   (B) "On the Warpath"
(C) "The Pirates Almost Go Home"   (D) "Sailing the
Seven Seas"

REMEMBERING DETAILS

2. What did the boys hunt after dinner?
(A) Turtle eggs   (B) Birds   (C) Rabbits   (D) Squirrels

3. After dinner Tom and Joe tried to
(A) dive   (B) smoke   (C) make smoke signals
(D) stand on their heads

4. What scared the boys in the middle of the night?
   (A) Intruders   (B) Wild animals   (C) A storm
   (D) Ghosts
5. What kept the boys from going home?
   (A) Tom's secret   (B) High tide   (C) A storm   (D) A discovery
6. Why did the "two Indians" not want to smoke a peace pipe?
   (A) They wanted to keep fighting.   (B) Smoking made them sick.   (C) They thought it was silly.   (D) They wanted to go home.

IDENTIFYING THE MOOD
7. What kept Tom from admitting he was homesick?
   (A) Fear   (B) Hatred   (C) Pride   (D) Excitement

THINKING IT OVER
1. What do you think Tom's secret was?
2. In what ways was Huck more grown-up than the others? Why do you think he was?

CHAPTER 17

FINDING THE MAIN IDEA
1. The main idea of this chapter is that
   (A) Aunt Polly takes Huck home   (B) the boys show up at their own funerals   (C) Saturday was a sad day
   (D) the funeral sermon was beautiful

REMEMBERING DETAILS
2. Everyone in the town felt sad about
   (A) the death of the three boys   (B) the damage caused by the storm   (C) Muff Potter's arrest   (D) the loss of the boat
3. When did the boys show up?
   (A) Before the service   (B) After the sermon   (C) Before the sermon   (D) After the service
4. How did most of the young people feel about Tom after he came back?
   (A) They laughed at him.   (B) They envied him.
   (C) They were mad at him.   (D) They felt sorry for him.

DRAWING CONCLUSIONS
5. Tom got slaps along with the kisses because
   (A) Aunt Polly had worried so much about him   (B) Aunt

Polly was sad to see him again   (C) Tom had ruined his
clothes   (D) Tom had interrupted the service

THINKING IT OVER

1. What are some of the funny points about the funeral? Why do
you think they are funny?
2. How do you think the townspeople felt about the boys
before they thought the boys were dead? Why did they change
their minds?

CHAPTER 18

REMEMBERING DETAILS

1. Tom's great secret was a plan to
(A) rob the house   (B) capture the steamboat   (C) run
away   (D) attend his own funeral
2. Aunt Polly blamed Tom for
(A) running away   (B) not telling her he was alive
(C) coming back   (D) stealing the ham
3. Tom's dream was so correct because
(A) he had really seen and heard everything   (B) Sid had
told him everything   (C) Aunt Polly had talked in her
sleep   (D) Tom could predict the future
4. Who spilled ink on Tom's spelling book?
(A) Becky   (B) Joe   (C) Sid   (D) Alfred

DRAWING CONCLUSIONS

5. Becky spent time with Alfred in order to
(A) read his comic book   (B) make friends with
him   (C) make Tom jealous   (D) show off

USING YOUR REASON

6. Instead of saying "their stories got bigger—and longer," the
author could have said
(A) more things happened   (B) the stories became
exaggerated   (C) the boys became writers   (D) the stories
were very dull

IDENTIFYING THE MOOD

7. How did Tom feel about Becky when he first came back?
(A) He forgave her.   (B) He was angry at her.   (C) He
thought he could live without her.   (D) He was sorry that he
worried her.

CHAPTER 19

FINDING THE MAIN IDEA

1. This chapter is mostly about how
   (A) Aunt Polly punishes Tom   (B) Aunt Polly forgives
   Tom   (C) Aunt Polly learns a lesson   (D) Tom fools
   Aunt Polly again

REMEMBERING DETAILS

2. How did Aunt Polly find out that Tom had lied to her about
   his dream?
   (A) She figured it out.   (B) Tom confessed.   (C) Sid told
   her.   (D) Joe Harper told her.

3. Aunt Polly thought that Tom had visited her in the night to
   (A) spy on her   (B) tell her he was alive   (C) steal some
   money   (D) laugh at her troubles

4. What did Aunt Polly find in Tom's pocket?
   (A) His bark note   (B) A piece of ham   (C) A silver
   dollar   (D) A knife

USING YOUR REASON

5. When Aunt Polly thought that Tom might have told a "good
   lie," she meant that Tom might have
   (A) lied to get out of trouble   (B) lied very convincingly
   (C) lied to make her happy   (D) believed what he said

6. Aunt Polly forgave Tom because she knew he
   (A) loved her   (B) was young   (C) would never change
   (D) didn't mean to lie

IDENTIFYING THE MOOD

7. Aunt Polly probably thought that Tom was
   (A) thoughtless but good   (B) thoughtless and cruel
   (C) cruel but honest   (D) thoughtful and honest

THINKING IT OVER

1. Do you think that Aunt Polly was the right person to raise
   Tom? Why or why not?

2. What do you think made Tom tell lies and hurt his aunt's
   feelings?

CHAPTER 20

FINDING THE MAIN IDEA

1. The main idea in this chapter is that
   (A) Tom gets whipped   (B) Becky gets whipped

(C) Becky fights with Tom   (D) Tom gets Becky out of trouble

REMEMBERING DETAILS

2. As soon as Tom met Becky he
   (A) apologized   (B) asked her to a picnic   (C) kissed her
   (D) tripped her
3. When Tom caught her reading the teacher's book, Becky
   (A) spilled ink on it   (B) wrote on it   (C) dropped it
   (D) ripped it
4. Who took the blame for harming the book?
   (A) Alfred   (B) Tom   (C) Amy   (D) Becky

USING YOUR REASON

5. Becky didn't tell Tom that Alfred had poured ink on his
   spelling book because she
   (A) forgot to   (B) wasn't sure who did it   (C) wanted to
   protect Alfred   (D) thought Tom would tell on her

IDENTIFYING THE MOOD

6. In the beginning of the chapter, how did Becky act toward
   Tom?
   (A) Thankful   (B) Cheerful   (C) Cold   (D) Admiringly
7. How did Becky act toward Tom at the end of the chapter?
   (A) Hostile   (B) Thankful   (C) Afraid   (D) Annoyed
8. This chapter shows that Tom could sometimes act
   (A) nobly   (B) cowardly   (C) thoughtlessly
   (D) selfishly

THINKING IT OVER

1. Why do you think Tom did what he did for Becky?
2. Good actions don't always *appear* to be good. What do you
   think Mr. Dobbins thought of Tom? Do you think he'd be
   surprised to learn how "noble" Tom had acted? Why?

CHAPTER 21

FINDING THE MAIN IDEA

1. This chapter is mostly about a
   (A) geography lesson   (B) parents' day at school
   (C) vacation   (D) church service

REMEMBERING DETAILS

2. The boys tried to get even with Mr. Dobbins by

(A) telling their parents (B) studying less (C) not coming to school (D) playing tricks

3. The audience laughed at the teacher because
   (A) he didn't know geography (B) he forgot a poem
   (C) a cat was hanging over his head (D) he tripped over the chair

4. What happened to the teacher's wig?
   (A) It was painted gold. (B) It was caught on a nail.
   (C) It was grabbed by a cat. (D) It caught on fire.

USING YOUR REASON

5. By saying the teacher "sat like a king on his great chair," the author suggests that Mr. Dobbins
   (A) wore a crown (B) felt important and powerful
   (C) looked noble (D) seemed tall

6. Mr. Dobbins became harder on his students because
   (A) their parents asked him to (B) he wanted to be a better teacher (C) he wanted them to impress their parents
   (D) they became more troublesome

THINKING IT OVER

1. How do you feel about the trick played on Mr. Dobbins? Was it cruel? Did he deserve it? Explain your answers.

2. Think about how the author felt about Mr. Dobbins. How do you think the author felt about people in powerful positions? Why do you think that?

CHAPTER 22

FINDING THE MAIN IDEA

1. This chapter is mostly concerned with
   (A) the Fourth of July (B) a circus in town (C) the slow summer days (D) summer picnics

REMEMBERING DETAILS

2. When Tom joined the Cadets he promised to
   (A) go to meetings on time (B) do good works (C) not tell club secrets (D) not smoke, chew, or swear

3. Tom fell ill with
   (A) measles (B) chicken pox (C) overwork
   (D) boredom

4. While Tom was ill, many of the boys in town
   (A) became religious   (B) made new friends   (C) formed another club   (D) told stories about Tom
5. Tom didn't feel so lonely when he saw
   (A) new boys in town   (B) two boys eating a stolen melon (C) two boys praying for him   (D) the boys marching in a parade

DRAWING CONCLUSIONS

6. Tom waited to repent because he didn't want to be a better boy
   (A) if he didn't have to   (B) before he talked to a minister (C) before he saw his friends   (D) unless he got over being sick

USING YOUR REASON

7. By saying that Tom was "lost, forever and forever," the author meant that Tom
   (A) didn't know where he was   (B) was still very sick (C) thought he was going to hell   (D) was forgotten by his friends
8. Tom joined the Cadets because he
   (A) wanted to impress Becky   (B) liked their uniforms (C) liked their rules   (D) wanted to help the sick
9. Tom was afraid of the storm because he thought it was
   (A) a dream   (B) a tornado   (C) a punishment   (D) the end of the world

READING FOR DEEPER MEANING

10. The author would probably agree that
    (A) human nature doesn't change   (B) people can change overnight   (C) storms are sent as warnings   (D) sickness can change people

THINKING IT OVER

1. Think of life in the village—without TV, movies, or cars. Do you think it was dull? Why or why not?
2. Tom found Jim Hollis "acting as a judge that was trying a cat for murdering a bird." What do you think the author means?

CHAPTER 23

FINDING THE MAIN IDEA

1. This chapter is mostly about

(A) Tom's promise   (B) Injun Joe's escape   (C) Huck's nightmare   (D) Potter's trial

REMEMBERING DETAILS

2. What excited the town?
(A) A circus   (B) The murder trial   (C) A robbery
(D) An election

3. Tom and Huck promised each other to
(A) tell the lawyer   (B) help Muff escape   (C) keep quiet
(D) go to the trial

4. Tom said on the witness stand that
(A) he hadn't seen anything   (B) a stranger killed the doctor   (C) Muff killed the doctor   (D) Injun Joe killed the doctor

5. What happened at the end of the chapter?
(A) Joe escaped.   (B) Joe was hanged.   (C) Muff was hanged.   (D) Huck told his story.

DRAWING CONCLUSIONS

6. When Tom was out late one night, he probably went to see
(A) Muff's lawyer   (B) Huck   (C) Injun Joe   (D) Muff

USING YOUR REASON

7. Instead of saying Muff was "of no account," Huck could have said that Muff
(A) was usually in trouble   (B) had no money   (C) was homely looking   (D) had too many children

IDENTIFYING THE MOOD

8. How did Tom feel about the trial?
(A) Excited   (B) Bored   (C) Curious   (D) Unhappy

THINKING IT OVER

1. Why were Tom and Huck afraid to tell the truth about Joe? What would you do if you were in their place? Why?

2. What do you think will happen to Joe? Will he get back at Tom for telling the truth? Will he ever be caught? Explain your answers.

CHAPTER 24

FINDING THE MAIN IDEA

1. This chapter is mostly concerned with how
(A) Tom felt about telling the truth   (B) Injun Joe planned

to get even   (C) the villagers formed a search party
(D) people felt about Tom

REMEMBERING DETAILS
2. Tom became famous in the town for
   (A) writing a newspaper article   (B) capturing Injun Joe
   (C) saving Huck   (D) freeing Muff
3. Tom wished he hadn't talked to the lawyer when he
   (A) saw Muff   (B) started to have bad dreams   (C) saw
   Huck   (D) met the reporters
4. Tom felt that he would never be safe until Injun Joe was
   (A) captured   (B) out of the country   (C) dead
   (D) forgiven

DRAWING CONCLUSIONS
5. Huck's part in the murder story was known to
   (A) no one but Tom   (B) everyone   (C) Injun Joe
   (D) the lawyer and Tom

USING YOUR REASON
6. Huck's confidence in human nature was wiped out because
   (A) people were mean to Muff   (B) Tom broke his promise
   (C) Joe escaped   (D) Tom got all the attention

IDENTIFYING THE MOOD
7. As the days drifted on, Tom began to feel
   (A) unhappier   (B) prouder   (C) less fearful   (D) more
   fearful

THINKING IT OVER
1. People were good to Muff now that he was out of trouble—
   just as they had forgotten him when he was in trouble. What
   does this suggest about how the author feels about human
   nature? Do you agree or disagree with him? Why?

CHAPTER 25

FINDING THE MAIN IDEA
1. This chapter is mostly about a
   (A) haunted house   (B) walk through the woods
   (C) hunt for buried treasure   (D) gang of robbers

REMEMBERING DETAILS
2. What did Tom want to look for?

(A) Buried treasure   (B) Injun Joe   (C)   Ghosts
(D) Huck's father
3. Who went looking with Tom?
(A) Ben   (B) Joe Harper   (C) Sid   (D) Huck
4. The last place they decided to look was in
(A) the Widow Douglas' home   (B) a haunted house
(C) the graveyard   (D) a forest

USING YOUR REASON
5. Huck didn't want to save his money because
(A) he wanted to spend it all on a horse   (B) he didn't
like money   (C) he wouldn't need it later on   (D) his
father would take it

IDENTIFYING THE MOOD
6. Huck felt that Tom was
(A) greedy   (B) distrustful   (C) trustworthy
(D) superior

THINKING IT OVER
1. When Tom decided to do something, like hunt for buried
treasure, do you think he really believed in what he was
doing? Why or why not?

CHAPTER 26

FINDING THE MAIN IDEA
1. This chapter is mostly about what the boys
(A) dug up under a tree   (B) met in the woods   (C) found
in the haunted house   (D) overheard in a tavern

REMEMBERING DETAILS
2. Where were the boys when the two men entered the house?
(A) Downstairs   (B) In the woods   (C) In the closet
(D) Upstairs
3. The boys were able to see the men through
(A) cracks in the floor   (B) a keyhole   (C) a window
(D) holes in the wall
4. Who was the deaf and dumb Spaniard?
(A) A fortuneteller   (B) Injun Joe   (C) The sheriff
(D) A peddler
5. What did the two men find under the floor?
(A) A skeleton   (B) A gun   (C) A pick   (D) A box of
money

6. Injun Joe did not catch the boys because
(A) they ran away   (B) the stairs fell through   (C) he couldn't see in the dark   (D) he fell asleep

DRAWING CONCLUSIONS

7. You can figure out that the boys didn't want to dig on Friday because they
(A) had to go to school   (B) had to do chores
(C) thought it was bad luck   (D) thought it was too hot
8. Joe was upset that the pick had fresh dirt on it because it meant that someone
(A) was ruining the garden   (B) hadn't cleaned it
(C) was snooping around   (D) had buried the money

THINKING IT OVER

1. Why were the boys surprised when they found out who the Spaniard really was? What do you think they will do about him? What would you have done? Why?

CHAPTER 27

FINDING THE MAIN IDEA

1. This chapter is mostly concerned with
(A) trailing Joe   (B) finding the treasure   (C) dreaming about the treasure   (D) looking for "Number Two"

REMEMBERING DETAILS

2. When Tom awoke, he wondered
(A) where the treasure was   (B) if the money had been stolen   (C) if it had been a dream   (D) where Huck was
3. What did Tom want to do about the treasure?
(A) Find it   (B) Tell the sheriff about it   (C) Leave it alone   (D) Help Joe hide it
4. The boys finally decided that "Number Two" was a
(A) house   (B) secret message   (C) box   (D) tavern room
5. If Joe returned, Tom wanted Huck to
(A) follow Joe   (B) call the sheriff   (C) call Tom
(D) ask Joe to give himself up

CHAPTER 28

FINDING THE MAIN IDEA

1. The main idea of this chapter is to tell

(A) how Tom tricked Joe   (B) what Tom found in the tavern room   (C) how Huck stole the treasure   (D) how much whiskey Injun Joe drank

REMEMBERING DETAILS

2. Who went into the tavern room?
   (A) Tom   (B) Huck   (C) Tom and Huck   (D) The tavern owner
3. What scared Tom?
   (A) A ghost   (B) A large cross   (C) Injun Joe   (D) The tavern keeper's body
4. What had happened to Joe?
   (A) He was murdered.   (B) He was tied up.   (C) He was sick.   (D) He was drunk.
5. Huck and Tom decided to steal the money
   (A) while Joe was sleeping   (B) when Joe wasn't there
   (C) when the storm broke   (D) while it was still daylight

USING YOUR REASON

6. The boys couldn't break into the room for a few days because
   (A) they were scared   (B) someone was watching them
   (C) it wasn't dark enough   (D) Joe was still in the room

THINKING IT OVER

1. Huck seemed to sleep anywhere he could—in barrels or in a barn. How do you think Huck felt about his homelessness? How would you feel? Explain your answers.

CHAPTER 29

FINDING THE MAIN IDEA

1. A good title for this chapter would be
   (A) "Lost in a Cave"   (B) "A Picnic and a Plot"
   (C) "Revenge at Last"   (D) "Looking for Treasure"

REMEMBERING DETAILS

2. People got to Becky's picnic by
   (A) foot   (B) steamboat   (C) horse   (D) train
3. Mrs. Thatcher thought that Becky would spend the night at
   (A) Susy Harper's   (B) Widow Douglas'   (C) Aunt Polly's
   (D) home
4. Tom asked Becky to stay at
   (A) Susy Harper's   (B) Widow Douglas'   (C) Aunt Polly's
   (D) Mrs. Thatcher's

5. During the picnic everyone explored
   (A) the woods   (B) an island   (C) the riverbank
   (D) a cave
6. When Huck saw the two men in town, he
   (A) called Tom   (B) followed them   (C) ran away
   (D) went into the tavern room
7. Injun Joe wanted to take revenge on
   (A) Widow Douglas   (B) Huck   (C) Tom   (D) Muff
8. When Huck heard Joe's plans, he
   (A) warned the Widow   (B) told Tom   (C) warned the
   Welshman   (D) told the Judge

USING YOUR REASON
9. Joe's partner agreed to the plan because he
   (A) hated the Widow   (B) was afraid of Joe   (C) wanted
   more money   (D) owed Joe a favor

THINKING IT OVER
1. The world of Tom Sawyer is mostly a happy one. Some
   people in the book have bad traits. But only one person is
   thoroughly evil. Who is he? Do you think he is true to life?
   Does he fit in Tom's small village? Explain your answers.

CHAPTER 30

REMEMBERING DETAILS
1. When the Welshman found Injun Joe, he and his boys
   (A) killed Joe   (B) captured Joe   (C) wounded both men
   (D) chased both men
2. Where were Becky and Tom?
   (A) In the cave   (B) At Mrs. Harper's   (C) At Widow
   Douglas'   (D) On the steamboat
3. The villagers knew where the children were because they
   (A) saw them   (B) heard them   (C) found clues
   (D) found a letter
4. Who searched for Tom and Becky?
   (A) Huck   (B) A few men   (C) Only their families
   (D) Nearly everyone
5. By the end of the chapter, Becky and Tom were missing for
   (A) a week   (B) three days   (C) overnight   (D) a day
6. What happened to Huck?
   (A) He disappeared.   (B) He became rich.   (C) He
   became sick.   (D) He became famous.

DRAWING CONCLUSIONS

7. The Widow started crying when Huck mentioned Tom
   because she thought that
   (A) Huck was dying   (B) Tom was probably dead
   (C) Huck was crazy   (D) Tom was a thief

USING YOUR REASON

8. Huck didn't want the Welshman to tell the widow that Huck
   had saved her because he
   (A) didn't like praise   (B) wanted to surprise her
   (C) didn't want Tom to know   (D) didn't want Injun Joe
   to know

THINKING IT OVER

1. How did the villagers act when there was an emergency? Do
   you think the people in your neighborhood would act the
   same way? Why or why not?

CHAPTER 31

FINDING THE MAIN IDEA

1. A good title for this chapter would be
   (A) "A Rescue"   (B) "Lost in a Cave"   (C) "Huck Gets
   Well Again"   (D) "The Search Party"

REMEMBERING DETAILS

2. Becky and Tom got lost in the cave because they were
   (A) playing a trick   (B) running away   (C) careless and
   confused   (D) chasing an animal
3. When they were hungry they ate
   (A) nothing   (B) cake   (C) apples   (D) candy
4. Their only source of light was
   (A) a flashlight   (B) sunlight   (C) a candle   (D) a
   bonfire
5. What did Tom find in the cave?
   (A) Injun Joe   (B) The search party   (C) A bear
   (D) Huck

DRAWING CONCLUSIONS

6. Tom shouted when he saw the candle because he
   (A) wanted to scare the person   (B) thought he'd be saved
   (C) was surprised   (D) was angry

IDENTIFYING THE MOOD

7. When Becky was in the cave she felt
   (A) happy   (B) angry   (C) rested   (D) frightened
8. How did Tom act in the cave?
   (A) He kept trying to escape.   (B) He was afraid to move.
   (C) He was too weak to walk.   (D) He was afraid of the dark.

THINKING IT OVER

1. Did you know that people could get lost in a big cave for days and perhaps never find a way out? Can you imagine what it must feel like? What would you have done in Tom's place?
2. What do you think of Becky's actions in the cave? Do you think all girls would act the same way? Why or why not?

CHAPTER 32

FINDING THE MAIN IDEA

1. The main idea of this chapter is that
   (A) the search party gives up   (B) Tom and Becky return
   (C) Huck gets better   (D) Injun Joe is caught

REMEMBERING DETAILS

2. How did Tom and Becky get out of the cave?
   (A) The search party found them.   (B) They followed Injun Joe.   (C) Some boatmen saved them.   (D) Tom found an opening in the cave.
3. Tom learned that Joe's partner had been
   (A) shot   (B) drowned   (C) arrested   (D) sick
4. Judge Thatcher had the cave
   (A) destroyed   (B) mapped   (C) guarded   (D) closed up
5. Tom almost fainted because
   (A) Injun Joe was trapped in the cave   (B) he was still weak   (C) Injun Joe had come back   (D) he was glad to be back

USING YOUR REASON

6. The men in the boat didn't believe that Tom and Becky were lost in the cave because
   (A) they were five miles away from the entrance   (B) the cave was too small   (C) they were so close to the entrance   (D) they weren't dirty

IDENTIFYING THE MOOD

7. When Tom and Becky returned, they were all of the following EXCEPT

(A) weak   (B) happy   (C) active   (D) hungry

THINKING IT OVER

1. If you were Tom, would you want to go back to the cave? Explain your answer.

CHAPTER 33

FINDING THE MAIN IDEA

1. The main idea of this chapter is that

(A) Joe dies   (B) the cave is sealed up   (C) the boys find the treasure   (D) the boys go to the widow's

REMEMBERING DETAILS

2. The people of the town found that Joe had

(A) been arrested   (B) killed himself   (C) starved to death   (D) been hanged

3. The boys found the money in the

(A) cave   (B) bank   (C) steamboat   (D) tavern

4. Tom got back into the cave by

(A) breaking through the door   (B) digging a hole

(C) crawling through a secret entrance   (D) rowing across the underground lake

5. Where was the "cross"?

(A) On Joe   (B) In the cave   (C) In the tavern   (D) In the strongbox

6. Mr. Jones brought the boys to

(A) the village square   (B) the widow's   (C) the church

(D) his house

USING YOUR REASON

7. Tom and Huck weren't afraid of Joe's ghost because

(A) they didn't believe in ghosts   (B) it was daytime

(C) the cross would keep it away   (D) Joe had only just died

IDENTIFYING THE MOOD

8. When Tom returned to the spring he felt

(A) excited   (B) calm   (C) troubled   (D) tired

THINKING IT OVER

1. Who do you think really owned the treasure? Do you think the boys should try to find the owners and return it? Why or why not?

CHAPTER 34

FINDING THE MAIN IDEA

1. This chapter is mostly concerned with what happened
(A) at the widow's party   (B) in the cave   (C) after the widow's party   (D) in the woodshed

REMEMBERING DETAILS

2. The widow was having a party to
(A) celebrate Joe's death   (B) thank the Welshman
(C) celebrate her birthday   (D) congratulate the treasure hunters
3. Mr. Jones' secret was that
(A) Huck saved the widow   (B) the treasure was found
(C) the boys would go to a good school   (D) the boys would get a medal
4. The widow wanted to thank Huck by
(A) sending him away to school   (B) giving him a home
(C) giving him a present   (D) paying him for his help
5. Tom surprised the party by
(A) playing a card trick   (B) telling a joke   (C) jumping out the window   (D) bringing in the money

USING YOUR REASON

6. Huck wanted to escape from the party because he
(A) hated crowds   (B) wanted to guard the money
(C) hated the widow   (D) thought he'd be punished

THINKING IT OVER

1. How do you think the people at the party felt when they saw the boys' treasure? How do you know?
2. What would you have done with the money? Why?

CHAPTER 35

REMEMBERING DETAILS

1. How were Tom and Huck treated by the villagers?

(A) They were ignored.   (B) They were admired.

(C) They were ridiculed.   (D) They were pampered.

2. The more the Judge got to know Tom, the more he became

(A) fond of him   (B) amused by him   (C) angry at him

(D) bored by him

3. What did the Judge plan to do with Tom?

(A) Take his money   (B) Send him away to camp

(C) Help him in a career   (D) Adopt him

4. At the widow's house, Huck was all of the following EXCEPT

(A) clean   (B) well-fed   (C) well-clothed   (D) happy

USING YOUR REASON

5. When he said "the widow eats by a bell," Huck meant she was

(A) hard of hearing   (B) very absent-minded   (C) on a
diet   (D) set in her ways

IDENTIFYING THE MOOD

6. Huck wanted to be

(A) rich   (B) free   (C) famous   (D) educated

READING FOR DEEPER MEANING

7. The author would probably agree that by living in a civilized
society we

(A) give up a lot of freedom   (B) become better people

(C) get more fun out of life   (D) live longer

THINKING IT OVER

1. Huck felt like a wild animal being tamed. Do you think living
in society would be better for him in the long run? Why or
why not?

2. How does Huck describe living in society? Do you agree?
Why or why not?

214